A LOVE UNBROKEN: A REGENCY ROMANCE

LANDON HOUSE (BOOK 3)

ROSE PEARSON

A LOVE UNBROKEN: A REGENCY
ROMANCE

Landon House

(Book 3)

By

Rose Pearson

A LOVE UNBROKEN: A REGENCY ROMANCE

CHAPTER ONE

Lady Selina Forrest sucked in a breath as she looked across the ballroom. She felt exposed and unprotected. Cold. This was not what she had expected to feel during the very first ball of the Season, but yet she could not remove such feelings. There was not even a glimmer of happiness within her, nor contentment or even interest! For whatever reason, she wanted nothing more than to turn around and make her way back to the carriage.

"Lady Selina?"

She started in surprise, then turned to Lady Hayward with a forced smile on her lips.

"Yes, Lady Hayward?"

There was no pretending when it came to Lady Hayward, however. The sharp look in her eye and the concern that was beginning to spread across her face told Selina that her chaperone was fully aware of what she was feeling.

"You are uncomfortable this evening?"

Selina closed her eyes for a moment and let out a long breath.

"Forgive me, Lady Hayward," she said, awkwardly. "I know that I am meant to feel excitement and all manner of happiness at being present this evening but, for whatever reason, I find myself pulling back from it."

Lady Hayward nodded, as though she had expected to hear such a thing from Selina.

"But that is understandable," she suggested as Selina frowned. "Surely you can see why? You must not berate yourself, my dear. It will just take a little time."

Not at all certain as to what Lady Hayward meant, Selina's frown deepened.

"It is not my first Season, Lady Hayward," she said, as if the lady needed to be reminded of it. "Last Season, I managed very well, did I not?"

Lady Hayward smiled and grasped Selina's hand.

"Forgive me, that is not what I meant to imply," she said, kindly. "What I meant to state, Lady Selina, is that this Season, you are present alone. You do not have your sister with you. It will take some time to adjust to such a circumstance, of course, but it is to be expected."

Selina hesitated, then nodded slowly, finally realizing what Lady Hayward meant. Swallowing hard, she looked all about her again, taking in the ball, the guests, the music, and the laughter which buzzed all around her. Last Season, she had found no difficulty in being present here but, then again, she had been standing with her twin sister, Lady Anna. In addition, Selina knew that Anna had a little more boldness than she, stepping forward whilst Selina herself lingered behind. Now, there was no Anna for her to remain behind, no shadow that she could hide herself in. Was that why she now felt as she did? Because she had no sister to hide behind?

"I did not mean to upset you," Lady Hayward said quietly, perhaps aware of the emotions that now ran amok in Selina's mind. "But only to encourage you not to believe that you are, somehow, expected to be something – or indeed, someone - you are not."

Selina took in a deep breath and tried to nod, understanding what Lady Hayward was saying but yet still feeling as though she ought to be thrilled with all that was going on rather than struggling to even remain in the ballroom! Looking about her, she took in another steadying breath and found her fingers curling tightly into fists as she tried her utmost to push away every last modicum of what she now knew to be fear. There was no reason to feel so, she told herself. She was with Lady Hayward, the lady who had guided both her twin sister and her older sister into happy marriages. Why then should she expect anything different for herself?

Because you lack the confidence your sister has.

Closing her eyes for a moment, Selina felt a tremor run through her. That was the truth and she could not deny it. Her twin sister Anna had always been the one to speak first, to smile first and to generally take the attention of whomever they had been conversing with. The confidence and assurance that Lady Anna always displayed was something that Selina herself was a little jealous of, given that she could not do the same. For whatever reason, however, she had never given her lack of self-assurance a great deal of consideration. It was only now, at this very moment as she stood in the ballroom, that she realized just how much she lacked.

"Lady Hayward, good evening!"

"Good evening, Lady Thurleigh," came the swift reply, as Selina turned quickly, ready to greet the lady in question. "And how do you fare this evening?"

Lady Thurleigh laughed, her eyes twinkling as she shook her head.

"You know how it is, Lady Hayward! I have spent almost every Season attempting to find a suitable match for my daughters, and now, finally, I find myself at the very last of them! I grow weary of it all, truth be told." Her gaze turned towards Selina, an enquiring look in her eyes. "And this must be your charge?" She glanced back to Lady Hayward. "I had heard that you had made some arrangement with the Duke of Landon, but I had not believed it!"

Lady Hayward smiled and introduced Selina, who quickly curtsied and kept her eyes low to the floor, finding herself a little embarrassed. Yes, it was true that Lady Hayward had made an arrangement with her father but for it to be spoken of so boldly and without any hesitation brought a touch of color to Selina's cheeks.

"The Duke of Landon has been very generous towards my son," Lady Hayward answered, quietly. "In addition, he has promised other benefits to the rest of my children, when the time comes, or when they are of age. In return, I am to bring his wonderful daughters into society, and do my utmost to guide them towards a suitable match." She twinkled up at Selina. "And thus far, I have not found my task to be an arduous one!"

This made Selina smile as Lady Thurleigh passed an assessing glance over her, as though deciding whether or not Lady Hayward would find it very difficult indeed to do the same for Selina.

"I see," she said, without malice or judgement in her voice but rather only interest. "Then I must wish you every success, Lady Selina – although my daughter must have her success too!" She laughed and Lady Hayward smiled back at Selina encouragingly. "I should introduce you to my daughter, in fact," Lady Thurleigh continued, as Selina remained standing quietly, finding very little to say. "I am sure she could do with another acquaintance and, given that the *ton* can be filled with insincere young ladies and the like, it can often be difficult to find a suitable friendship." Another assessing glance swept over Selina, leaving her feeling quite vulnerable. "I am sure that you are *not* insincere, however, given that Lady Hayward is your chaperone and guide, Lady Selina. Might you wish to meet Lady Prudence? Ah, look! She is coming now."

Selina, who had opened her mouth to answer and then closed it again given that Lady Thurleigh was about to introduce her daughter regardless of what Selina said, turned quickly so that she might greet the lady warmly, only to see a gentleman approaching them, a young lady on his arm. Her eyes lifted to the gentleman's face, finding his piercing blue eyes suddenly resting upon her also. Blushing furiously, she looked away at once, realizing just how handsome the gentleman was and cursing her own foolishness.

"We are returned, Lady Thurleigh!" the gentleman exclaimed, as though Lady Thurleigh had expected otherwise. "I do hope you saw the dance. It was an excellent quadrille, I must say."

As Selina allowed herself another glance, she saw the gentleman bow over Lady Prudence's hand, before finally releasing her. A streak of heat ran down her spine as he looked towards her again, but this time, she forced herself not to look away.

"I did not observe you for a great length of time, I am afraid," Lady Thurleigh replied, with a chuckle. "I saw an old acquaintance of mine and had to come and speak to her almost at once!" Turning to Lady Hayward, she quickly introduced her. "And this is her charge, Lady Selina, daughter to the Duke of Landon." With a warm smile on her face, Lady Thurleigh gestured to the gentleman. "Lady Selina, this is the Earl of Barrington and, alongside him, my daughter, Lady Prudence."

Gathering herself, and pulling her gaze away from the gentleman, Selina curtsied quickly.

"Good evening to you both," she answered, hating that her voice was so very quiet indeed. "I am pleased to make your acquaintance."

She did not look back at Lord Barrington, quite certain that, should she do so, her face would flush terribly and he would know just how handsome she thought him. Instead, she looked towards Lady Prudence as she rose, smiling at her briefly before placing her hands together in front of her and glancing towards Lady Hayward, who was smiling serenely.

"Lady Selina, I am very glad to have met you," Lady Prudence said hastily, taking a few steps closer to Selina as though she was truly delighted to have been introduced. "To be truthful, I am the very last daughter of my family to have a Season and, as such, have no family present with me, save for my mother! All my other sisters came with each other, whilst I was left waiting!"

"Is that what you call gratitude?" Lady Thurleigh interrupted, her voice high pitched as she glared at her daughter. "There is nothing but complaint with you!"

"No, mama," Lady Prudence answered, quickly. "What I really meant to express was..."

Selina did not listen to the girl's explanation. Instead, she looked once more to Lord Barrington, taking in the way his eyes danced with both good humor and interest as he observed mother and daughter. He had broad shoulders and stood tall and strong, with startling blue eyes and light brown hair which was swept neatly to one side of his forehead. When he smiled at something Lady Prudence said, something curled in Selina's stomach – and she once more found a flush coming to her cheeks and berated herself silently for it. The *ton* was filled with handsome gentlemen, and she was expected not only to be introduced to them, but also to converse, dance and entertain them, upon occasion. She could not permit herself to have such a reaction as this simply because a handsome gentleman came into her view!

I have not behaved this way before.

Frowning, Selina recalled how, last Season, she had

been able to talk and dance with any gentleman who asked her, without any real difficulty whatsoever. Again, it might well have been because her sister had been present with her and had, therefore, managed most of the conversation and the like. Now, standing here without anyone by her side, without her sister and her overflowing confidence, Selina realized just how weak she truly was.

"Might you care for a dance, Lady Selina?"

It took Selina a moment or two to realize that the conversation between Lady Thurleigh and Lady Prudence had come to an end. Not only that, it took her another few moments to realize that Lord Barrington was now addressing her, looking at her with an enquiring gleam in his eye.

"My – my dance card," Selina murmured, as heat poured into her face. "Yes, yes, of course, Lord Barrington. I – " Fumbling with the ribbon, she finally managed to release it from her wrist and handed it to him, aware of the small smile on his face as she did so. "You will find it quite empty, Lord Barrington, as we have only just arrived."

"I am sure it will not be so for long," came the quick reply, as he bent his head to look it over. Knots began to tie themselves in Selina's stomach as she waited, aware of just how ridiculous she must have sounded to the gentleman. For her first ball of the Season, she was not managing to behave with any sort of poise or elegance. Rather she was making an utter fool of herself.

"The cotillion?" Lord Barrington asked, looking up at her, one eyebrow raised slightly. "Would that suit you, Lady Selina?"

"Yes, of course," she managed to say, as Lady Hayward looked on. "Thank you, Lord Barrington."

He smiled at her.

"But of course." Handing her back the dance card, he bowed low. "And now I should excuse myself. The scotch reel is soon to be upon us and I am to dance with Miss Arbuckle."

Selina dropped into a curtsey, relief filling her as the gentleman took his leave. Their conversation, for the moment at least, was entirely at an end.

"Lord Barrington is *very* handsome, is he not?"

A little startled, Selina looked towards Lady Prudence, who was watching the gentleman leave with a soft smile on her face, as though she were deeply invested in the gentleman's company and was now sorry to have to lose it for a time.

"I am only glad that he came to ask me to dance before the rest of my dances were taken!" She laughed and looked meaningfully towards Selina, who found herself inwardly recoiling. "He has asked me for *two* dances, in fact. The second is to be within the hour, although I must say I am not certain what to do with his attentions, should they increase, for I have many other gentlemen eager to dance with me." Again, her eyes pierced Selina's. "Did he only choose the one dance with you, Lady Selina? That is unfortunate." A long sigh left her lips and she shook her head, as though Selina lacked something that she herself had but could not impart. "You must try to make a better impression upon gentlemen, Lady Selina, for perhaps then, they might –"

"As Lady Selina has said, my dear, she has only just

arrived," Lady Thurleigh interrupted hastily, in a clear attempt to prevent her daughter from saying anything more. "But yes, of course, Lord Barrington is *very* handsome and most eligible too, I might add!"

Lady Hayward put a hand on Selina's arm. "Perhaps a glass of wine or champagne?" she asked, changing the subject entirely. "Or should you like to make your way through the guests so that we might greet those that we are acquainted with?"

Selina, seeing the glint of steel in Lady Hayward's eye and knowing full well that she was just as displeased with Lady Prudence's words as Selina was, smiled at her chaperone.

"Might I suggest we do both?" she asked, as Lady Hayward nodded. "As you say, we should greet those that we are acquainted with, given that it is my first outing into society since we returned to London." With another swift smile, she bobbed a quick curtsy towards Lady Thurleigh and Lady Prudence. "Pray excuse me."

Lady Thurleigh's expression was one of distress, perhaps because she was aware that her daughter had been the one to chase Selina away, given what she had said.

"I am sure we will meet again very soon," Lady Hayward said kindly, as Lady Thurleigh remained silent, her brow furrowing as she shot a hard glance towards her daughter. "Thank you for your conversation, Lady Thurleigh. It has been very good to see you again." Lady Hayward turned to Lady Prudence, who had gone a little pale, perhaps anticipating the anger that would soon follow from her mother, once Selina had gone. "Good evening, Lady Prudence. I have been glad to make your acquaintance."

"As have I," Selina lied, before turning on her heel and beginning to walk away.

Lady Hayward joined her.

"Good gracious!" she exclaimed, the moment they were out of earshot. "I did not think that Lady Prudence would be so rude! To speak with such impropriety is more than a little embarrassing, and I should think that Lady Thurleigh will have sharp words to say to her daughter, once we are gone from their company." Selina shot a quick glance behind her and saw Lady Thurleigh speaking quickly to her daughter, her shoulders lifted and an anger evident in her expression. Lady Prudence was standing quietly, her head bowed and her shoulders lowered as she accepted her mother's berating. "Whilst you might believe you need a little more confidence, Lady Selina," Lady Hayward added, "to be *overly* so is also a trait that requires... consideration."

Selina shook her head, letting out a long breath.

"I think Lady Prudence wanted to make certain that I knew just how successful she had been with the gentlemen of the *ton*," she said, as Lady Hayward nodded. "I cannot understand why, but –"

"Because you are the daughter of a Duke," Lady Hayward interrupted, with a small smile. "She is the daughter of an Earl and, whilst that title is not to be ignored, it fades a good deal when placed beside that of a Duke. That is all."

Frowning, Selina let out a long breath.

"I see."

"It might well be difficult to gain acquaintances that have not a single ounce of jealousy within their hearts," Lady Hayward warned. "I am aware that both you and Lady Anna depended on each other's company somewhat, and I suppose that your sister had the advantage of your presence with her, given that she wed first. However, that does not mean that we will not be able to discover the very best of company for you, my dear." Her eyes twinkled as she glanced towards Selina. "And that includes the very best of gentlemen."

A wry smile caught Selina's lips.

"And if I continue to make a fool of myself in front of such gentlemen?" she asked, as Lady Hayward laughed. "For whatever reason, I could not even remove my dance card from my wrist when Lord Barrington asked!"

Lady Hayward laughed again, and Selina's heart lightened just a little, pulling itself away from the despair and the upset that had filled it only some moments ago.

"Do not think that you will struggle for the entirety of this Season, Lady Selina," Lady Hayward replied, after a moment or two. "At the first few social occasions you might find yourself a little overwhelmed, a little awkward or even a little embarrassed at times, but soon all such feelings will fade away and you will discover a confidence within yourself that you were not aware of before."

Selina looked towards her chaperone, finding her heart eager to believe it, but her head refusing to do so.

"Are you quite certain, Lady Hayward?" she asked, as her chaperone nodded firmly. "I fear that I shall remain this uncertain, unsure, young lady for the rest of the Season and that I shall have to return to my father's estate without any sort of success."

"Nonsense," Lady Hayward replied, looking towards Selina with a firm and steady gaze as she turned towards her. "You will find yourself quite at your ease in a few days' time. I am quite sure of it."

CHAPTER TWO

"What is this?" Charles gestured to a pile of bills that now sat in the middle of his desk, as his sister gazed at them without any flicker of understanding in her eyes. "Amelia!" Charles barked, growing more and more irritated with her. "Might I ask you what the meaning of these are?"

Amelia lifted her eyes to his, a bored expression on her face.

"I do not understand what you mean, Barrington," she said calmly, as though spending a great deal of money was to be expected. "I required some new items and thus, the accounting for such items was sent to you for payment." She tilted her head and looked up at him, bird-like. "Is that a difficulty for you?"

Charles bit back his first, angry response, knowing full well that his sister would not take such a sharp answer with any degree of understanding. She was a proud, conceited young lady and, try as he might,

Charles simply could not get her to understand why he disliked her behaving so.

"Amelia, you have just had an entire new wardrobe purchased for you," he reminded her, keeping hold of his fraying temper as best he could. "You have multiple new gowns, which are all of the highest fashion. You have had all of the trinkets which a lady could require given to you, with new gloves, jewelry and bonnets all purchased." He gestured to the stack of bills. "Why then would you consider purchasing yet *more* items without even speaking to me first?"

He had looked through each one of the bills and had found his anger growing steadily as he had done so. They had all been fripperies, as far as he was concerned. All items that his sister did not need, but had chosen to purchase regardless – and all without so much as a by-your-leave! Had she come to him, had she expressed to him that she desired such things then, of course, he would have listened to her, but he might also have been able to dissuade her from such nonsense.

Closing his eyes, Charles took in a long breath. Why had he been left with a sister who thought of nothing and nobody but herself? Why had she been placed as a burden upon *his* shoulders when she ought to have wed their cousin, as he was sure had been arranged? Charles was still unclear as to why the match had never taken place, since it had been expected to occur before his father had passed away, a little over a year ago, and it was not as though Amelia herself would discuss it with him!

"It is just one or two additional items, brother," Amelia said, her voice becoming something akin to a whine. "You have a great fortune, do you not? These things are nothing to you."

"That is not the point of this discussion, Amelia!" he retorted, swiftly. "I will not have you telling me that you have decided to order things such as these whenever you wish! From now on, you are forbidden from making any sort of purchase without discussing it with me first."

Amelia did not instantly respond. Her eyes, so cool and clear like their mother's, gazed back at him.

"Mama says –"

"Mama does not hold the purse strings," Charles reminded her, his brow furrowing as another flare of anger took hold of his heart. Had his mother been the one to encourage Amelia to do this? There was little doubt that she wanted the very best for her daughter and, if that meant allowing Amelia to make her way to the milliners and place an order for various items she *supposedly* required, then he expected that their mother would concede, perhaps even encourage her. "If you wish to remain in London, Amelia – and be reminded that I am the one who will decide whether or not you stay for the Season – you will heed me and do as I ask!"

These words, more than any other, seemed to have an effect on his sister. With wide eyes, she looked back at him, her face paling as she realized what he meant.

"You would not do such a thing!" she whispered, as if attempting to find the courage to stand up to his harsh words. "I know you would not! Mama –"

"Enough, Amelia!" Charles rose from his chair and placed his hands firmly on the desk, looking across at his younger sister and finding his temper no longer contained. "I have heard quite enough. *If* I decide that it is best for you to return to the estate, then I shall do so regardless of what our mother states. You may believe that you have come to London to do as you please, but that, I will remind you, is not at all the situation you are in. Everything from your pin money to your lady's maid is under my control." He swallowed hard, disliking the fact that he had to remind his sister of such a thing, but knowing that it was best for her that he do so. "Everything that you have required has been given to you without hesitation. You have the very best of things, Amelia, but if you continue to behave in this imprudent, unconsidered fashion, then I will have no choice but to return to the estate and take both you and mama with me." Keeping his gaze steady and ignoring the tears that had sprung into her eyes, Charles thumped one hand on the table for good measure. "Is that quite clear, Amelia?"

His sister jerked visibly and one hand went to her mouth as a single tear fell to her cheek. Charles remained unmoved, waiting for her acknowledgement as he stood silently, still fixed and determined in his gaze.

"Yes, Barrington."

Her words were quiet, her voice low as she dropped her head, another tear splashing onto her hand as she sat, the picture of obedience, in her chair.

"You are dismissed."

Charles waited for his sister to take her leave, refusing to be drawn into her theatrics and making it quite plain by the hardness in his voice and the firmness of his stance that he would not accept any sort of foolishness from her. These last two weeks had been nothing but a trial and he was not about to allow it to continue any longer.

With a sniff, Amelia pulled out her handkerchief and dabbed at her eyes before slowly rising from her chair. The swish of her skirts was the only sound as she made her way from the room, taking her time to walk past his desk and sniff once more, her handkerchief still in her hand. Charles set his jaw firmly, and narrowed his eyes, everything within him tightening until, finally, the door closed behind her.

Letting out a great sigh, he flung himself back in his chair and closed his eyes, feeling the tension flood out of him as he did so. He would have to speak to his mother next, but that could wait for a short time, although certainly it would have to be done by the close of the day. No doubt she would make a great fuss of what he had said to Amelia and would attempt to berate him for his harsh words, but Charles was utterly determined to do as he had said. If his sister continued to behave in such a fashion, then it would be best for her to return home, so that she might consider her behavior and improve it for the following year. She was young enough and there would be plenty of time for her to enjoy the Season and find a match! He need not feel any sort of guilt over the matter.

After spending some time making certain that his sister's debts were paid – for what he determined would be the last time for this Season – Charles was about to ring for some refreshments when Jamison, his butler, tapped on the door.

"Enter."

The butler did so, and handed Charles a card, then stood and waited for his instructions.

"Lord Banfield!" Charles exclaimed, handing the card back to the butler. "Yes of course, and at once! From now on, if Lord Banfield calls, he is to be shown in immediately."

Jamison acquiesced and, in a few moments, Lord Banfield stepped into the room.

"Banfield!" Charles exclaimed, coming around from his desk to greet his old friend. "How very good to see you! I did not know that you had returned to London!"

Lord Banfield chuckled and nodded.

"For my sins, yes, I have," he replied, his jolly face lighting up as he shook Charles' hand. "Only two days ago, however. I thought I should write to inform you of my return, but then decided to call instead."

"I am very glad you did so," Charles replied, conducting his friend to a chair. "Brandy?"

"Of course!" Lord Banfield exclaimed, making Charles laugh. "You always seem to have the most excellent brandy, whereas my own dulls in comparison."

Charles handed his friend a glass, then sat down in a chair opposite and let out a long sigh.

"You look a little weary, old friend," Lord Banfield said, quietly, observing Charles for a moment. "Has something in London troubled you?"

Charles smiled ruefully.

"I have been in London for two Seasons, I think," he said slowly, as his friend nodded. "Last Season, I was absent, as you know, due to the mourning period for my father." He let out a long breath. "This Season, however,

I have my sister with me in London and, with her, our mother."

Lord Banfield's eyes flared for a moment only, then he began to chuckle as he took in Charles' depressed expression.

"Forgive me," he said, one hand pressed against his heart. "I should not laugh when you are clearly in distress!" With an effort, he quelled his mirth. "Is it a great trial?"

Charles closed his eyes and let out a groan.

"It is good you have returned to London," he said, honestly. "For you will be able to advise me."

"Advise you?" Lord Banfield spluttered, his eyes widening. "I have no advice to give, Barrington!"

"You have sisters!" Charles argued, but Lord Banfield shook his head.

"They are all older than I, if you recall," he said, firmly. "I was not required to lead them through society, to find them suitable matches." He shrugged. "My father passed away many years ago, as you well know, but by then, my eldest two sisters were already wed, leaving me with the younger two. My mother swiftly found matches for them and the situation was brought to a most satisfactory conclusion without any requirement for my involvement."

Rolling his eyes, Charles picked up his brandy and took a sip.

"Then you can be no help whatsoever," he said, with a heavy sigh. "Already, my sister – who has only just made her debut, I might add – has become demanding, thoughtless and, I confess, a little arrogant." Quickly, he related what had occurred with the bills that had been given to him by the various shopkeepers whom his sister had visited, seeing the way Lord Banfield's eyes widened. "She has been given many new gowns and all manner of things," he finished, "but yet believes that she still requires more."

Lord Banfield ran one hand over his eyes and sat back in his chair.

"I can offer you nothing save to say that what you have done thus far, I believe, is a wise course of action. She will not thank you for it at present, of course, but you must continue to be firm."

"Thank you," Charles replied, raising his glass in a mock toast before taking a sip. "My mother, unfortunately, appears to be very much on the side of my sister and will, of course, make her feelings on the matter known to me very soon. I fully intend to be quite clear with her also, of course, knowing full well that she *also* will not appreciate my attempts to steer Amelia in the right direction." He let out a long breath and shook his head. "The sooner I find her a match, the better."

Lifting his brows, Lord Banfield looked back at him.

"You mean to say that you shall not allow her any choice in the matter?"

"I fully intend to allow her to enjoy the Season, if that is what you mean," Charles replied. "But I do not think that she will be able to make any sort of wise decision when it comes to the gentlemen of the *ton*. Most likely, she will be drawn to a most unsuitable sort and I shall have to insist that he is not appropriate for her and then face the consequences of such a decision!" Rolling his eyes, he sighed with frustration. "Would that I was here in London alone!"

"Ah, the responsibilities that come with the title," Lord Banfield replied, with a grimace. "I myself am come to London in the hope of securing a future for myself." He cast a quick glance towards Charles and then looked away, clearing his throat as though embarrassed. "I mean to find a bride."

Charles' eyes widened and he sat up a little straighter in his chair.

"You?" he repeated, as though he could not quite believe what he had heard. "You seek a bride?"

"I must," Lord Banfield answered with a small shrug lifting his shoulders. "If I am to continue the family line, then it is expected of me. With no younger brother to claim the title should anything happen to me, then it would all go to a most undeserving cousin who, I believe, is simply praying for the day that I might fall from my horse or be shot in a duel." He winced and picked up his brandy. "It is important that I marry."

A sudden thought slammed into Charles' mind and he could not help but chuckle.

"I do have a sister who is looking to make a match," he said, as Lord Banfield laughed. "If you are struggling to find a match, then might I suggest her to you?"

"After all you have told me of her, after the many claims you have made of her arrogance and her thrifty ways, I hardly think you have encouraged me!" Lord Banfield laughed, as Charles winced. "But I shall, of course, make certain to dance with her during a ball or two. She is your sister after all."

"And I am sure she will be very grateful for it."

Lord Banfield lapsed into silence for a few minutes, then gestured with his brandy towards Charles.

"And you?" he asked, all trace of mirth gone. "I know you have been busy with your sister's debut but have you any thought of matrimony? Is there any young lady amongst the *ton* who has caught your attention?"

Charles shook his head.

"None," he replied, his lips twisting. "Last evening I was in the company of Lady Prudence – do you recall her? This is her third Season, I believe, so she must certainly be looking for a husband! Her mother, despite her best efforts, has been unable to curb that young lady's tongue. She speaks much too fondly of herself, flirts outrageously and does nothing at all to endear herself to anyone." With a small shrug, he threw back the rest of his brandy. "But it means very little to me, given that I have no intention whatsoever of marrying this Season. No, I am determined to give all of my attentions and my energy to my sister, so that *she* might find contentment and, in doing so, bring the very same to me also!"

Lord Banfield grinned.

"I will pray you have success," he replied. "Now, would you like to join a small gathering I am to have in a few days' time?"

Charles looked at him in surprise.

"Already? You have organized such a thing within only two days of being in London?"

"I am to find a wife, am I not?" Lord Banfield replied, as though Charles ought to realize why such a thing made sense. "Therefore, I ought to be doing all I can to meet eligible young ladies and deciding which of them I might consider. I am not about to rush into any sort of betrothal without making sure that I am quite certain of the lady in question and that, my friend, takes time."

"I quite understand," Charles replied, with a grin. "Then yes, of course, I should be glad to join you."

"And your sister and mother also, of course," Lord Banfield replied, making Charles groan audibly. "Come now, you cannot think that I would only invite yourself to such a gathering! What would your mother think of me?"

"I cannot escape them, it seems," Charles replied, with a shake of his head. "Very well, I shall, of course, take them with me."

"Capital!" Lord Banfield boomed, as Charles felt his heart slowly sink to the floor with dismay.

This Season would certainly be very different to the others he had enjoyed before.

CHAPTER THREE

"It is very generous of you, Lord Banfield, to invite me." Selina rose from her curtsy and tried to smile at Lord Banfield, who merely laughed and shook his head.

"Not at all, Lady Selina!" he cried, bowing low. "It is my honor to have you here this evening. And you also, Lady Hayward."

"Lord Banfield." Lady Hayward curtsied as she greeted him and then smiled. "I am very glad to see you again. Has London been favorable for you thus far?"

Lord Banfield laughed again, his eyes twinkling.

"I have only been in London for less than a fortnight, Lady Hayward, but certainly, I have enjoyed being back in society again. Particularly when there is such fine company to be had."

His eyes turned back to Selina and she found herself blushing, relieved when Lady Hayward took her leave of Lord Banfield and they made their way further into his drawing room.

Lord Banfield was an Earl, from what Selina

recalled, and a man of very good character also. Last Season, when they had been introduced, there had been no particular interest on her part and, it seemed, on his either, but she had been glad to know him. Therefore, this evening, she felt a little more at ease, praying that she would not embarrass herself in any way. Over the last few days, she had found social occasions to be a little easier and had managed to relax just a fraction, although certainly she found them still trying. She had never truly realized just how much she had come to rely on Anna's presence by her side, had never understood just how much she needed her. Now that she was alone, she felt a deep failing of confidence in herself, and that left her severely lacking compared to the other young ladies of the *ton*. She was not a wallflower by any means, but neither was she the confident, assured young lady that she was expected to be by the *beau monde*.

"Look, there is that gentleman you danced with during your first ball of the Season!" Lady Hayward said quietly, gesturing with her fan towards the man Selina remembered to be Lord Barrington. "I am sure that he will converse with you, should you wish it."

Selina swallowed hard. It took strength of character to merely make one's way towards a group in the hope that they would be willing to greet her. If they did not, then she would be forced to turn to her right and attempt such a thing again. Lady Hayward appeared to be quite confident in the belief that Lord Barrington would not only recall her, but greet her, which was not something Selina herself believed. She doubted, was fearful, and already embarrassed at the mere thought of being ignored.

"Ah, Lady Selina!"

Looking over her shoulder, Selina let out a long breath of relief as Lord Banfield came towards her, evidently having something further to say.

"You recall Lord Barrington, do you not?" he said, walking alongside her towards the gentleman, whose eyes quickly darted towards Lord Banfield before glancing at her. "Lord Barrington, might you introduce your sister to Lady Selina? I am sure that Lady Amelia would be glad of a new acquaintance."

Selina caught her breath as Lord Barrington frowned. Was he displeased with her in some way? Had she made such a poor impression upon him during their first meeting that he did not want her to be anywhere near his sister?

"Good evening, Lord Barrington," she managed to say, bobbing a quick curtsey. "You remember Lady Hayward?"

"Your chaperone, of course," he said, bowing towards Lady Hayward and then to her. "Good evening to you both." His frown had lifted and no longer did he appear at all irritated with her, as she had feared. "Might I introduce my sister to you, Lady Selina?"

"Of course."

Selina smiled at the young lady in question who, much to her surprise, had something of a disdainful look on her face. There was a flash of irritation in her eyes, as though she was upset that Selina had decided to interrupt her conversation with her brother.

"Amelia, mother, might I introduce Lady Selina Forrest, daughter to the Duke of Landon," Lord Barrington said, gesturing to Selina. "Lady Selina, this is my sister, Lady Amelia." He turned to an older lady to his left. "And my mother, Lady Barrington."

"How very good to meet you both." Selina curtsied quickly, noting with surprise that Lady Amelia's expression had changed almost at once. "And this is my chaperone, Lady Hayward."

Once all of the introductions had been made and a few words of greeting exchanged, Selina allowed herself another look towards Lady Amelia. No longer was there any sort of disdain in her eyes, no look of frustration or irritation but rather, instead, a keen awareness of who Selina was.

"Lady Selina, I am so very glad to make your acquaintance," Lady Amelia said, as Lady Hayward was drawn into conversation with Lady Barrington, although Lord Barrington remained silent.

Lord Banfield had melted back into his crowd of guests, leaving Selina to converse with Lady Amelia.

"Have you been in London for long?" Selina asked. "I have only been present for a fortnight or so myself."

"As have I," Lady Amelia replied, her eyes bright and her smile ready on her lips. "I must say, Lady Selina, I do not know very many other young ladies in London as yet. I should very much like it if we could become better acquainted."

Selina smiled, although her heart became a little sorrowful. She had slowly begun to realize that Lady Amelia's change in expression and manner had come solely from the realization that Selina was the daughter of a Duke - and that fact did not please her very much at all. Was Lady Amelia somewhat arrogant in her status as the daughter – and now sister – of the Earl of Barrington? If that was the case, then Selina did not think that she wished to develop any sort of friendship with the lady.

"Tell me," she began, changing the subject entirely and refusing to state anything that might sound like an agreement to do as Lady Amelia had suggested. "Have you found society to be welcoming toward you? I do hope so. A debut year can be very exciting indeed."

Lady Amelia clasped her hands together and gave a deep, contented sigh.

"Oh yes, very much indeed," she gushed, quickly going into a long, extended speech about all that had occurred and just how much she had enjoyed it all.

Selina listened as best she could, but slowly became aware of Lord Barrington watching them, his brow lowered and his eyes a little sharp. Daring a glance at him, she saw his expression quickly change as she caught his eye, perhaps causing him, only then to realize that he had been watching them both with such intensity. He cleared his throat, his brow lifted, and the tightness left his jaw. Whatever it was that had been troubling him, he quickly hid it, leaving Selina wondering just what it was about her company that seemed to displease him so.

"I do hope that we might take tea together some day, Lady Selina," Lady Amelia finished, reaching out to touch Selina's arm for just a moment, drawing her attention back to the lady. "I am sure we will become very good friends indeed."

Selina murmured something indistinct and smiled, just as another young lady came to approach them. Without seeming to even pause for breath, Lady Amelia turned away from Selina and grasped the hands of the young lady, turning so swiftly that Selina was left looking at the vacant space where Lady Amelia had stood only moments before.

She blinked her astonishment away, composing herself, and making certain that no expression of surprise remained on her face before turning towards Lady Hayward in the hope that they might extricate themselves from Lord Barrington's company altogether. Given that Lord Barrington had frowned at her, evidently displeased with her company, and now Lady Amelia had turned away from her so quickly, Selina was both embarrassed and a little frustrated. She had no understanding as to why Lord Barrington appeared so, and certainly Lady Amelia had behaved in a rather rude fashion also. They did not know of her struggle to make her way in society with confidence of course, but certainly she was not inclined to remain in their company any longer.

"Lady Selina," Lord Barrington rumbled, catching her attention. "I –"

"Ah, Lord Barrington!"

Another voice came from over Selina's shoulder and, in an instant, she found herself swiftly removed from whatever conversation Lord Barrington had intended to have with her, replaced with a young lady and her mother who practically pushed Selina out of her way as she drew close to Lord Barrington. Selina did not hear what was said, her face beginning to burn with embarrassment as she finally caught Lady Hayward's eye. Thankfully, her chaperone seemed to understand Selina's distress and took her leave of Lady Barrington quickly, coming to Selina's side as they bid the lady good evening.

"Are you quite all right?" Lady Hayward asked urgently, as they made their way across the room and through the door into the adjoining music room, which had been opened for the guests also. "Is something wrong?"

Selina did not immediately answer, taking in quick breaths in the hope of composing herself further before she chose to respond. Lady Hayward did not hurry her, waiting quietly until Selina was ready to speak.

"Lady Amelia was not at all eager for my company until she learned that I was the Duke of Landon's daughter," she said slowly, as Lady Hayward frowned. "She made it quite clear that she would be very pleased if we could continue our acquaintance, but I find that I am not inclined towards it."

"That is perfectly reasonable," Lady Hayward said, but Selina had not finished speaking, finding her embarrassment now turning to anger. It was not an emotion she often felt, but now that it had taken a hold of her, it began to lick hot flames all through her heart.

"Whilst I was conversing with Lady Amelia, Lord Barrington did nothing but frown heavily at us both," she continued, her own brows lowering. "As though to state that he was displeased with my company! Lady Amelia, however, then displayed a great rudeness of manner in turning away from me the moment another young lady of her acquaintance came towards her, only for Lord Barrington, who seemed about to speak to me, to then be distracted in much the same way."

Lady Hayward sighed and shook her head.

"I am sorry to hear what occurred," she said, gently, "but mayhap Lord Barrington's frown was not aimed towards you, my dear."

Selina glanced at her. Lady Hayward's calm words had quietened her anger somewhat, although her face was still flushed and a tension still ran through her frame.

"What do you mean?"

"It may have been his sister," Lady Hayward suggested, as Selina's brows knotted once more. "Mayhap he was displeased with her over some matter that we are, as yet, unaware of, and that contributed to his expression as he watched and listened to the conversation."

It was not something that Selina had considered, but the fact that Lord Barrington had been so quickly distracted by the young lady and her mother, rather than continuing what he had been about to say to her, only confirmed that he, as far as she was concerned, was just as rude as his sister.

"Aside from such difficulties, I think you did very well," Lady Hayward went on, clearly now trying to encourage Selina. "Your confidence when you are amongst society is continuing to grow."

Selina allowed her shoulders to slump as she looked towards Lady Hayward, seeing her smile at her and yet feeling a deep despondency within her heart.

"I am not like Anna," she said, quietly, as Lady Hayward's smile faded. "Would that I was."

"Why should you think that?" Lady Hayward asked, sounding quite surprised. "As I have said to you before, Lady Selina, you are not required to be your sister! There is nothing wrong with the person you are."

"But I wish I had as much confidence and assurance as she has!" Selina exclaimed, surprising herself with just how fervently she spoke. "I am nothing but a mouse, shrinking back from those who surround me. Instead of reaching out, instead of greeting those I am acquainted with, I wait until they recognize me, for fear that they will not be glad of my company should I step forward. It was never so with Anna! She was always willing, always eager to make her presence known to others, and she reaped the benefits of it!"

Lady Hayward took Selina's hand in her own and turned towards her, looking at her firmly.

"Lady Selina, I have never seen any fault in your manner nor your character," she said, as Selina swallowed hard, feeling sudden tears flood into her eyes. "You may feel as though you lack confidence, but I can assure you that you have done very well indeed these last few weeks. You do not need to replicate your sister in every way. She is your twin, yes, but that does not mean that your characters must be similar also! I will promise you that, should you attempt to model your behavior on that of Lady Anna, you will find yourself filled with distress and frustration, for you will be merely playing a part rather than allowing those around you to see you as you truly are." Her hand let go of Selina's, but not before she had given it a gentle squeeze. "If you are to find a suitable match, Lady Selina, then do you not want the gentleman in question to know your character as it is? To allow them to believe a pretense will bring no happiness to either of you."

"But I dislike my shy nature," Selina replied, her voice breaking with emotion. "I want very much to be as Anna is."

Lady Hayward shook her head.

"You equate confidence with success," she said, softly. "That is not so. I have seen many a young lady – and I speak of wallflowers here, Lady Selina – who have found themselves very happily settled with a gentleman of their choice. The gentleman in question is usually much as they are: quiet in nature, thoughtful and reflective. Can you imagine how difficult it would be for such a lady to pretend to be a gregarious, vivacious character, only to wed a gentleman who believed her to be so? She would have a constant struggle to keep up such a pretense, never once being able to reveal her true nature to him. That cannot bring happiness, Lady Selina. That cannot bring contentment. Find satisfaction and gladness with the character that you have and do not force yourself to take on your sister's traits in the hope that it will improve you somehow. I assure you, it will not."

Selina let out a long breath, nodded and looked down. She felt weak and tired, and suddenly had a very strong urge to return home.

"How can I be sure?"

"Trust me. Come with me," Lady Hayward said gently. "I can see that you need a few minutes to rest. There is a quieter corner here where we might sit."

Allowing Lady Hayward to lead her across the room,

Selina took in long, steadying breaths and forced any tears that had attempted to return to her away once more. She had not meant to let out such an explosion of words such as she had done, but something about Lady Amelia and Lord Barrington had practically forced the words from her. She was very blessed indeed to have Lady Hayward as both her companion and her chaperone, for she was a lady who was filled with understanding and wisdom, who knew precisely what to say and how to encourage her. And yet Selina continued to fight the urge to be as Anna was, to try to find a way to feign the confidence that she had so often seen in her twin sister. But the truth was that, as hard as it was to admit even to herself, she was more reserved than Anna. She was quieter and inclined to be a little distant, even from her own family at times. Was it true that she might still be able to find a good match with her character such as it was? Her heart struggled to believe it.

"Now, I shall go and fetch us both something to drink," Lady Hayward said, as Selina sat down in a chair, relieved to no longer be standing. "I will only be a few moments."

Selina nodded and sat back, glad to have a few minutes of respite in which to gather herself. Her gaze roved aimlessly over the crowd of guests, seeing so many laughing and conversing together, clearly enjoying the evening.

There were none like her, she noted. None standing silently, their eyes downcast or sitting alone as they waited for someone to come and join them. Her heart sank a little lower – only for a frown to flicker across her brow as she saw none other than Lady Amelia and her friend, whom she had greeted when Selina had been still conversing with her. They walked quickly into the music room, their heads close together and, much to Selina's surprise, no sign of Lord Barrington or Lady Amelia's mother present with them. As she watched, the two young ladies came to a slow stop, only a short distance away from where she sat, still conversing and laughing together as they did so. Thinking that Lord Barrington or Lady Barrington would soon come to join them, Selina turned her gaze away, telling herself that it was none of her business what they spoke of or how they acted. It was only when another passing glance revealed that a gentleman had come to join the two ladies that her worry began to increase.

The gentleman in question was someone Selina did not know. He bowed to first one lady and then the other, although, as far as Selina was concerned, he stood a little too close to Lady Amelia. Her breath caught as she saw him run his hand down Lady Amelia's arm, catching sight of the blush that spread over Lady Amelia's cheeks as he did so. When he took Lady Amelia's hand and brought it to his lips – with the other young lady giggling like a foolish child – she found herself on her feet and making her way directly towards them.

"Lady Selina?"

The voice filled her with relief.

"Lady Hayward," Selina said quickly, never taking her eyes from the scene before her. "How glad I am that you have returned." She took the glass of wine from Lady

Hayward without even looking at it. "Please, might you join me?"

Lady Hayward nodded, although the confusion on her face was more than evident.

"But of course. Why –"

"Lady Amelia has found herself in a less than proper situation," Selina said, as Lady Hayward looked in the direction that Selina was watching – and Selina heard her swift intake of breath. "Might we join them?"

"Of course." Lady Hayward started forward at once, not allowing even a moment of hesitation. "Where is Lord Barrington? Or her mother?"

"I do not know," Selina answered, her voice low. "Nor do I know the gentleman, but I thought it best we join them."

Lady Hayward threw her a quick, admiring glance.

"Very considerate of you, Lady Selina," she said, before clearing her throat, lifting her chin and placing a broad smile on her face.

"Lady Amelia!" she exclaimed, as the gentleman suddenly took a few steps back, a look of panic catching his eyes as both Lady Hayward and Selina came to join them. "I did not get a moment to speak to you when your brother introduced us. Forgive me." She looked all about her, feigning confusion. "Where is your brother at present, Lady Amelia?"

Much as Selina had expected, Lady Amelia blushed furiously and dropped her gaze.

"We must have left him with another," she said, halt-ingly. "I – I did not notice, given that I was speaking to my dear friend, Miss Newington." She gestured to the young lady beside her. "Miss Newington, this is Lady Hayward and Lady Selina Forrest, daughter to the Duke of Landon."

Miss Newington – a young lady with very pale blue eyes, a sharp nose and cheeks that were entirely absent of color at present – dropped into a quick curtsey, although she said nothing at all, clearly aware that both she and Lady Amelia had been seen in the company of a gentleman without a chaperone beside them.

"And this gentleman you were conversing with?" Lady Hayward asked, one brow lifting as she turned to the yet unnamed stranger. "Might you introduce us also, Lady Amelia?"

A coldness came into her eyes as Lady Amelia hastily introduced one Lord Telford and Selina was all too aware of Lady Amelia's flushed cheeks, as well as the gentleman's clear embarrassment. He bowed and murmured a greeting to both Selina and to Lady Hayward, only for his eyes to flare as he caught sight of someone – or something – just to Selina's left. She turned and, to her relief, saw none other than Lord Barrington approaching.

"Do excuse me," she heard Lord Telford say, turning back to see him bow low. "I shall leave you to your conversation."

"How very strange," Lady Hayward murmured, as Lord Telford hurried away. "I do hope that he –"

"Amelia!"

The Earl's furious voice crashed between them, ending Lady Hayward's words and making the group, as a whole, turn towards them.

"Barrington," Lady Amelia replied, her voice a little

hoarse as she tried to smile at her brother, although Selina could see the wariness in her eyes. "We – we must have wandered off without realizing you were not with us. I –"

"Did I see Lord Telford conversing with you?" he interrupted, speaking directly to his sister as though Selina and Lady Hayward were not present. "I have told you before that such a gentleman must be entirely ignored, no matter how many words of flattery he puts before you."

Selina, who still thought Lady Amelia most unwise and believed that she had deliberately escaped her brother in order to have a conversation with Lord Telford, turned towards Lord Barrington a little more.

"If I might, Lord Barrington, Lord Telford was only in your sister's company for a few moments," she said, a little surprised at how confidently she was speaking. "Lady Hayward and I joined them very soon after he drew near."

Something flickered in Lord Barrington's eyes, although he swiftly inclined his head by way of thanks.

"Then I am relieved to know that no harm has come to my sister or to her *friend*," he replied, shooting a hard glance towards Miss Newington, who had dropped her gaze to the floor and kept it there. "It was foolish of you, Amelia, to walk away as you did. I do hope that you have expressed your own gratitude to Lady Selina and Lady Hayward for coming to your aid."

Lady Amelia's color heightened all the more, and she lifted her chin, her eyes a little narrowed as she returned her brother's hard stare. For some moments, she said nothing, her lower lip curled in defiance – but evidently, the anger in her brother's eyes was enough to force her to capitulate.

"I thank you," she murmured eventually, dropping into a quick curtsey as she turned to Lady Hayward and to Selina. "As I have said, we must have accidentally left my brother's company without realizing it. I am very grateful that you came to join us when Lord Telford was present."

Selina, who did not believe a word that came from Lady Amelia's mouth, nodded and then forced a smile to her lips.

"But of course," she said, as Lady Hayward caught her eye. "We shall leave you to your conversation now. Good evening."

"Good evening," Lady Hayward added, turning on her heel and coming to join Selina as they made their way back to where Selina had been sitting.

"Goodness," Lady Hayward murmured. "It appears that Lord Telford is a gentleman we must be wary of, Lady Selina. Lord Barrington certainly appeared to think so!" She smiled at Selina as they sat down together, with Selina's eyes drifting back towards Lord Barrington, who was now, it seemed, quietly berating his sister all over again. "You did very well, Lady Selina. I commend you for your concern and for your actions."

Selina shook her head.

"I am sure anyone would have done such a thing," she answered, seeing how Lady Amelia now dropped her head, no longer staring defiantly back at her brother. "I do hope that he is not too harsh with her."

"I hope that he is!" Lady Hayward replied, with a

small smile. "I believe that Lady Amelia is the sort of young lady who will do whatever she wishes without hesitation, unless she is checked. And that, Lady Selina, is a sure path to disaster and disgrace."

Letting out a long breath, Selina sat back in her chair and nodded, surprised that there was no longer any weakness or fatigue in her limbs. Rather, she now felt like rising to her feet and joining the other guests, so that she might converse with them. Perhaps being in Lord Barrington's company and forcing herself to speak with both confidence and strength had done her more good than she had at first realized!

"Lord Barrington was grateful to you," Lady Hayward murmured, as Selina frowned, catching Lady Hayward's knowing look. "He might well come to seek you out again to thank you once more, the next time we are at the same social occasion as he."

Laughing, Selina shook her head.

"He may very well do so, Lady Hayward, but I highly doubt that he will have any genuine interest in me, and certainly I have none for him!" Recalling how he had frowned at her when she had first been talking to Lady Amelia, as well as the way that he had allowed himself to be dragged into conversation with someone else rather than finish what he was saying to Selina, she shook her head again, although with a little more fervor this time. "I shall be quite glad to know Lord Barrington, certainly, but there will be nothing more than an acquaintance between us."

"Are you quite certain of that?" Lady Hayward asked, but Selina nodded her head.

"I am," Selina declared, with a small smile lighting her lips. "And for myself, I shall state that I have no interest in furthering an acquaintance with him regardless." She looked across the room at him once more, taking in his dark expression, his heavy brows and the firmness about his mouth. "No, certainly not," she murmured, half to herself. "Such a thing shall never be. I am certain of it."

CHAPTER FOUR

Charles cleared his throat, grasping both his mother and his sister's attention. They glanced at each other, and Charles was well able to see the fear in his sister's eyes.

He did not care. Whatever his sister had said to their mother, whatever excuses they had devised together, he was not about to allow such a thing to happen again.

"Last evening," he began, slowly, "you chose to step away from both myself and mama, in order to pursue conversation with a gentleman who, I am sure you are fully aware now, is entirely unsuitable." Amelia said nothing, although she did hold his gaze rather than drop it to her plate or to her lap. Charles was not certain whether or not he ought to be irritated by this, wondering silently if his sister was about to defend herself to him yet again. "Lord Telford, I believe, came to speak to you for the sole purpose of settling himself into your affections," he continued, one hand curling into a fist as he spoke. "Whilst I had no choice but to introduce you at last week's ball – for he approached, if you recall, and expressed a keen desire to know you – that does not mean that he is a gentleman whom you should further an acquaintance with."

His mother shook her head.

"Your sister did not know such a thing, Barrington," she said, reproachfully. "How can she understand such an important matter if you do not take the time to explain it?"

Charles looked to his sister and saw a faint touch of color come into her cheeks.

"That is where you are mistaken, mama," he said, quietly. "I *did* explain this to Amelia. I informed her of it, last week at the ball, the moment Lord Telford departed, as well as once more, when we returned home." He smiled grimly as he saw his mother's eyes flare and a small exclamation leave her lips. Whatever Amelia had said to her was now being proven to be quite incorrect. "Is that not so, Amelia?"

His sister let out a heavy sigh and shrugged.

"I do not know," she stated, with a glance towards her mother. "There have been so many gentlemen that it is difficult for me to recall them all."

"That is not the truth and you well know it," Charles replied, grimly. "You deliberately left my side last evening to go with your friend in the hope of speaking to Lord Telford. Is that not so?"

"Amelia!" their mother exclaimed, turning in her chair to look at her daughter, her upset now all the more evident. "You told me that you were entirely unaware of Lord Telford's unsuitability and that it was quite by chance that you were in his company once more. In fact," she continued, her voice rising higher and higher, "you stated that it was your friend, Miss Newington, who drew you towards him."

At this, Amelia dropped her head, no longer any trace of defiance about her.

"I have already warned you, Amelia, about your conduct," Charles continued, a little more gently. "First of all, you purchase items without even asking me whether or not such a thing is permitted, and now you throw aside my company and mama's companionship in order to escape to another part of the room, so that you might be in the company of a gentleman who wants nothing more from you than the dowry you would bring to the wedding."

Lady Amelia lifted her head sharply.

"That is not true," she stated, angrily. "Lord Telford was most attentive. He –"

"He is practically insolvent!" Lady Barrington interrupted, before Charles could speak. "Do you not understand, you foolish girl?" She slammed one fist down on the table, making the crockery tremble and her daughter stare at her, wide-eyed. "I believed you when you stated your meeting was entirely accidental - and now, I discover that you have told me untruths!"

"I – I just wanted to speak to him!" Lady Amelia stammered, looking from her mother to Charles and back again. "There is nothing wrong with that desire, surely?"

"There is when you are forced to practically run away from your brother!" Lady Barrington exclaimed, her anger and upset still clearly visible in her words and her expression. "I trusted your words, Amelia, only to now realize just how foolish I have been!"

Charles found his heart filling with relief as he saw the way that his mother now spoke to his sister. He had believed that Lady Barrington would present herself before him with the intention of defending Lady Amelia's actions, only to now see that his mother was very upset indeed. He was not glad for her upset, of course, but he was certainly relieved that she was not attempting to defend Amelia's actions. Evidently, she was fully aware of the sort of gentleman Lord Telford was, and could see the danger that had been so very close to Amelia.

"You did find them in time, I hope?" his mother asked, turning wide eyes towards Charles, her voice filled with desperation. "There were not any others who noticed him speaking to my daughter unattended?"

"They might well have done, had it not been for Lady Selina Forrest and Lady Hayward," Charles replied, solemnly. "When I approached, it was with such relief and gladness to see them both standing with Amelia. Lord Telford took his leave the moment he saw me approach, which is yet another reason for you to realize just how unsuitable he is, Amelia!"

"I did not ask for her company," Lady Amelia replied, ungratefully. "I knew Lady Selina had seen us, but I did not think she would bring Lady Hayward to join us. We were simply having a conversation, Barrington!" Her head lifted slowly and she looked back at him, a flicker of resentment growing in her eyes. "I thought it a little rude that they both forced their company upon us!"

"Then you are even more of a fool than I first thought," he responded swiftly, as their mother shook her head, closing her eyes for a long moment. "Can you not see just what Lady Selina and Lady Hayward did for you, Amelia? By having Lady Hayward's company, she made the gathering quite respectable. No doubt she would have lingered beside you until I or Mama came in search of you. You cannot know just how grateful I am to them both."

"Nor I," Lady Barrington added, passing one hand over her eyes before she pushed herself up from the table, her desire to eat evidently gone entirely. "Barrington, I have thought you too harsh with your threat to return Amelia to the estate, should she continue on with such silliness," she continued, standing behind her chair now and looking at him. "But now that I have heard the truth of this, now that I have come to realize just how much of a fool I have become in trusting my daughter's words, I no longer think you too severe."

"Mama!" Lady Amelia gasped, turning her head to look at her mother, but Lady Barrington remained firm.

"If such a thing should happen again, Amelia, I will personally put you in the carriage myself and have us both driven back to the estate," Lady Barrington said, glaring at her daughter. "Your brother can remain here, if he so wishes, for there is no need for him to forgo the rest of the Season on your account!" She looked back at Charles, who nodded his head, appreciating her determination and her willingness to now come alongside him in encouraging Amelia to behave properly. With a deep breath, she delivered the last part of her proclamation.

"This is your only warning, Amelia. Anything more and I shall have our bags packed and your Season will be at an end."

"Thank you, Mama," Charles said quietly.

Lady Amelia rose from her chair, one hand balling up her napkin as tears flooded her eyes. She made to say something, opening and closing her mouth many times before, finally, with a strangled sob, she rushed from the room.

"I do not mean to upset her so," Charles said, softly as Lady Barrington made her way to the door. "But you must understand that it is for the best, Mama."

She looked back at him, her face set and her coloring still rather pale.

"Have no fear," she replied, shaking her head. "I understand everything now, Barrington. Your sister made a very severe mistake last evening."

"Are you going to go after her?" he asked, but Lady Barrington shook her head.

"I am going to write to Lady Hayward," she responded, with a small smile. "I wish to thank her for keeping my daughter safe from Lord Telford's advances last evening, and to inform her that such a thing will never happen again."

Charles nodded, but said nothing more, waiting until his mother had closed the door behind her before he allowed himself to flop back in his chair, a long and heavy breath escaping him. Closing his eyes, he recalled all that had occurred last evening. He had been most displeased with Amelia's conduct from the very beginning, finding her looking all around her with an air of dislike.

When Lady Selina and Lady Hayward had come to join them, there had been such a curl of disdain on his sister's face that he had wanted to drag her to one side and berate her furiously. It had been all the more irritating to see her so changed when she realized just who Lady Selina was, for she had immediately become eager to be in her company, glad to converse with her and doing all she could to further their acquaintance – although Charles suspected that Lady Selina herself was not particularly eager for such a thing.

Opening his eyes, he reached for his coffee and finished it quickly, trying to find the force of will needed to remove himself from the table and continue on with all that he had to do but, for whatever reason, he could not harness the impetus to do so. Instead, he found himself weary and deflated. The look on his sister's face had been one of utter dismay, but Charles did not regret what he had said nor what his mother had said either. It was a relief to have Lady Barrington agreeing with him, for he had feared that he would have both his sister *and* his mother fighting against him.

"Mayhap I should write to her," he mused, tilting his head as he considered.

If his mother was to write to Lady Hayward to thank her for all she had done last evening, then mayhap his duty was to do the same for Lady Selina. From what Amelia had said, it seemed that Lady Selina had been the one to notice both herself and Miss Newington from the first, who perhaps had alerted Lady Hayward, who had then hurried to join them. Regardless, he felt as though she was deserving of his thanks.

Forcing himself from his chair, Charles made his way from the dining room to his study, finding a great sense of peace wash over him as he closed the door tightly behind him, leaning back against it for a moment. Quite how he was to continue helping Amelia when she was so determined to do as she pleased, he did not know. He could only hope that this would be the moment she realized that she could not continue to behave in such a manner.

Making his way to his desk, he sat down heavily and looked blankly at the papers in front of him. When he had looked all about him last evening and realized that his sister was gone from his company, he had felt such a rush of fear that he had been unable to move for a moment or two. Having no wish to upset his mother, he had made his way through the ballroom, looking all about him in as surreptitious manner as possible. When he had seen her in the music room, his heart had slammed hard against his chest, noticing Lord Telford stepping back from them at once. A mixture of relief, gratitude, anger and disappointment had warred within his heart and he had been forced to use every last part of his resolve to keep his voice steady as he spoke to his sister.

Lady Selina had watched quietly, her expression serene and yet her eyes filled with an awareness of what might have been. He certainly owed her a great deal.

Pulling out a fresh piece of parchment, Charles picked up his quill and found his ink bottle. And then, he began to write.

∾

"Good gracious!"

Charles looked up from where he had been sanding his letter to Lady Selina, seeing his friend standing in the doorway.

"Ah," he replied, a little awkwardly. "Do come in, Banfield. Ignore this mess, I beg you."

Clearing his throat, he glanced at the tray to his right, where nuncheon had been set for him. He had forgotten to eat even a single thing, such had been his concentration on the letter.

Jamison, who was holding the door open for Lord Banfield, made to come in, clearly eager to help Charles tidy the mess that he himself had created, but Charles waved him away.

"It is but a few sheets of parchment," he said, as the butler's eyes remained fixed on the floor. "I am more than able to place them in the fireplace. Please, attend to your duties."

Jamison nodded and stepped away, pulling the door closed behind him and leaving Lord Banfield staring at the many crumpled up sheets of paper that littered not only Charles' desk but also the floor around it.

"I have been attempting a letter," Charles said, by way of explanation. "It has been proving difficult to put my thoughts into words."

"I can see that," Lord Banfield replied, as Charles folded up his letter, ready to seal it. "It must be a letter of great importance."

Charles nodded, rising from his chair and collecting up all of the other letters which he had started and then thrown aside.

"Indeed," he said, without giving any further explanation. "I shall burn these at once. You will not mind?"

Lord Banfield chuckled and shook his head.

"Might I ask to whom you are writing?" he asked, a slight gleam coming into his eye. "A young lady, mayhap?"

Picking up the strewn pieces of paper that lay across his desk, Charles let out a bark of laughter.

"You are correct, Banfield. I am indeed writing to a young lady – but not for the reasons you yourself might believe!"

"Oh?"

Lord Banfield's brows rose, indicating that he did not quite believe Charles.

"My sister put herself in a very foolish position last evening," Charles replied, grimacing. "It was no-one's fault but her own and, unfortunately, was deliberately done. However, she was rescued from this particular situation by Lady Selina Forrest and her chaperone, Lady Hayward, who came to join both her and her friend as Lord Telford spoke to them."

Lord Banfield's face dropped, all expression of mirth gone.

"Telford?" he repeated, as Charles nodded, grimly. "That man is nothing more than a rogue. Your sister must be informed of his –"

"I informed her of his reputation the very same evening that they were introduced, over a week ago" Charles replied, with a shake of his head. "Miss Newington, who I believe is one of my sister's particular friends, has clearly a penchant for Lord Telford and, together, they made their way from my company and from my mother's company also, so that they might speak with Telford. I am very grateful to Lady Selina for noting the situation, and stepping forward at once, along with Lady Hayward. Together, they made certain that the situation remained entirely proper and, at the same time, prevented Telford from perhaps saying or doing whatever he intended to, towards either my sister or Miss Newington."

Nodding slowly, Lord Banfield gestured to the papers that Charles had yet to pick up from the floor.

"And therefore, you have been writing to Lady Selina, simply to thank her?"

"That is what I was attempting to do, yes," Charles replied, coming around in front of his desk to pick up the last of the papers. "It has taken me a good many attempts to write an expression of thanks that I find to be suitable. It was difficult also not to make my sister out to be the most ridiculous and foolish of young ladies, even though I am fully aware that she is so!"

"And, no doubt, Lady Selina will be aware of it also, given that she saw what occurred," Lord Banfield pointed out, as Charles threw the rest of his papers on the, as yet unlit, fire. "But you have found something to write that is satisfactory to you, I hope?"

"I have," Charles replied, quickly setting the papers alight and standing back so that they might begin to burn. He did not want any of his staff coming into his study to see the papers sitting there, for no doubt a nosy maid or two might attempt to read one and know precisely what had happened to his sister. "I have asked if I might call upon her to express my thanks in person." When he turned back, Lord Banfield was looking back at him with a small, knowing smile tugging at the corner of his mouth. Charles frowned. "You need not think that there is any more to my wish to thank her, save for my own feeling that it is required," he said firmly, knowing all too well what his friend was thinking. "That is all."

"Lady Selina is a very kind young lady, it appears," Lord Banfield replied, a trifle airily. "To not only take note of your sister's situation, but also to step forward so that she might protect Lady Amelia says a great deal about her character. Besides which, she *is* the daughter of a Duke!"

Charles rolled his eyes.

"I have no intention towards matrimony, as you well know," he said, reminding his friend of what he had said in previous discussions. "I have enough on my mind at present regardless, given my sister's continued foolishness!"

"And your mother?" Lord Banfield asked, quietly, looking at Charles with interest. "Does she continue to side with your sister?"

"Thankfully, she does not," Charles replied, sitting back down, but keeping one eye on the flames in the grate, wanting to make certain that everything was burned up. "I believe that Amelia was rather taken aback, truth be told! My mother was horrified to hear what had occurred and has stated that she will return Amelia to the estate should such a thing happen again." He grinned broadly at his friend. "Whilst I, it seems, will be permitted to remain here to enjoy the rest of the

Season. My mother has, I must confess, surprised me with her determination to steer Amelia towards the right path. I thought she might make all manner of excuses for her."

Lord Banfield nodded, stretched languidly and then pushed himself out of his chair.

"I am off to take a short walk in the park," he declared, looking meaningfully at Charles. "Do you wish to join me?"

Charles laughed aloud, knowing precisely what his friend intended.

"You mean to say that you want to greet those all about you who might have heard of the success of your little soiree last evening, in the hope of, perhaps, either continuing or forming an attachment with a young lady of quality?"

He laughed all the more when his friend's face slowly darkened, his mouth settling into a flat line.

"That may be so, but need I remind you that I am determined to wed this Season?" Lord Banfield replied, a little tersely. "I must do all I can to make myself appear eligible and a suitable prospect to the ladies of the *beau monde*!"

"And that requires taking a short walk through the park?" Charles asked, as Lord Banfield nodded fervently. "Do you mean to say that there was no-one at your soiree who caught your attention? None that you might wish to call on this afternoon?"

Lord Banfield sighed heavily.

"None," he said, a little more quietly. "Although mayhap I should give a little more attention to Lady

Selina, given just how highly I now come to think of her, after what you have told me."

Making to answer in the affirmative, Charles was surprised when he found himself frowning, lines forming across his brow and his stomach twisting in a most uncomfortable fashion. Of course he should encourage Banfield in such an endeavour! Why would he not? There was no possible reason for him to feel such a way, and so he dismissed it as quickly as he could, clearing his throat and pushing himself out of his chair in an attempt to hide the truth of what he felt.

"That may well be a good suggestion," he replied, as Lord Banfield eyed him carefully, evidently aware that it had taken a few moments for Charles to answer. "I am sure that she would be an excellent match for you."

Lord Banfield did not say anything in response to this, merely watching Charles for another moment or two before he shrugged, sighed and made his way to the door.

"Might you wish to join me?" he asked again, as Charles hesitated. "It is a very fine day and you might find that the afternoon air does you good." He chuckled. "Removes some of the stress and strain that you feel at present!"

Charles considered for another moment or two. He had been thinking of his sister for most of the morning, it seemed, although he wondered if he ought to remain in case his mother should require him. Amelia might become very upset indeed, and he would have to step in.

However, he thought, tilting his head just a fraction, his mother had enough fortitude of her own when it was required. He had seen the flash of anger in her eyes that very morning and was sure that she would now be making quite certain that Amelia knew just how much she had disappointed her.

"Very well!" he exclaimed, as Lord Banfield grinned. "My sister will not be permitted to set foot outside the door this afternoon, I believe, so there is no reason for me to remain. And as for this evening's ball, I am not at all certain that my mother will still be content for her to attend!"

"Then I pity you for the distress and upset that will follow, should such a thing occur!" Lord Banfield replied, with a grin. "And suggest to you that it is all the more reason why you might decide to join me this afternoon."

"Indeed," Charles agreed, suddenly feeling a good deal more at ease. Picking up the letter to Lady Selina, he took it with him with the intention of giving it to one of his footmen to deliver. "You are quite right, Banfield. Let us take a walk in the park and see if I cannot forget about this whole, wretched business for a short while!"

CHAPTER FIVE

The note Selina had received from Lord Barrington was, whilst unexpected, very welcome indeed. She had found herself smiling a little as she had read his many gracious and grateful words, although when she had read the part where he begged to call upon her soon so that he might express his thanks to her in person, heat had seared its way up her spine and sent color pouring into her cheeks.

Lady Hayward had not been present at the time, which Selina was glad of indeed, although her father had been in the same room as she – thankfully quite caught up in his own reading. The Duke of Landon was not a gentleman inclined towards noticing his daughters a great deal. Whilst she knew that he loved her and, of course, she in return loved him, there was not a closeness between them. That was why she considered herself so very grateful for Lady Hayward. These last few weeks, the lady had become something of a confidante and had encouraged Selina significantly. That did not mean, of course, that Selina's confidence had grown to the point where she felt at ease during social occasions, but certainly, there was the beginning of the acceptance within her heart that she was not ever going to be as assured as her sister, and that such a fact was not a bad thing.

"Lady Hayward," she murmured, as the carriage drew near to Lord and Lady Folkstone's townhouse. "I should inform you that I received a letter from Lord Barrington this afternoon." Lady Hayward's expression was half hidden by the shadows of both the carriage and the gloom of the early evening, but Selina knew that she would be very interested indeed. "He wrote mainly to thank me for what occurred with his sister," she continued, before Lady Hayward could say anything. "I believe that Lady Amelia must have seen me approaching her, as well as how I spoke to you also, as I continued." She waved a hand, surprised at the slight nervousness that filled her. "Regardless, he was very grateful and wishes to call upon me to thank us both in person."

"That is very generous of him," Lady Hayward commented, without any other inflection in her voice. "I do hope his sister is quite all right. She was rather unwise in her choice of company."

"I know nothing of Lord Telford, nor of Miss Newington," Selina replied, as the carriage trundled on. "Is there any sort of difficulty with either of them?"

Lady Hayward sighed audibly.

"Miss Newington, I do not know much about, whereas Lord Telford is known to have a very poor reputation indeed. I should be very glad if you would remain far from him, Lady Selina."

Selina nodded fervently.

"Of course," she agreed, not wanting to disagree for a moment. "I am sorry that he made his way to Lady Amelia's side, then. How disgraceful!"

"Do not think that he was not welcomed," Lady Hayward replied, with a shake of her head. "I am certain that both of those young ladies thought him excellent company and might well have sought him out!"

"But why should they do so?" Selina asked, horrified. "Surely they would know of his reputation?"

"Because," Lady Hayward replied, with a heavy sigh, "some young ladies like the attention that a rogue will give to them. They find it delightful to be in his company, to have him flirt with them and compliment them so highly that they can do nothing but blush and giggle. It is only themselves that they place in danger, however, for a rogue can have words that are so smooth that these young ladies are often pulled away from their own sensibilities."

Selina closed her eyes and drew in a long breath.

"Then I am all the more glad that we spoke to Lady Amelia when we did," she replied, fervently. "And I am sure, given what Lord Barrington wrote to me, that he will have spoken to Lady Amelia of it also."

Lady Hayward nodded, the carriage coming to a stop as footmen hurried to open the door for them.

"I should think he would have done," she agreed, with a wry smile. "And I do not think he would have held back his upset from her either which, I would state, is precisely what Lady Amelia requires."

Nothing more was said on the matter as Selina and Lady Hayward made their way up towards the house. There was a slight chill in the air, but Selina barely felt it, her anticipation and nervousness growing in equal measure. This evening, she would be required to dance with, and converse with, various gentlemen of the *ton* and, whilst most young ladies would revel in such an experience, Selina felt some anxiety building up within her. She prayed that she would not falter during any of the dances, that she would be able to converse without difficulty and that her nervousness would not show to any of those she spoke to that evening.

Will Lord Barrington be present?

The question came, unbidden, to her mind and Selina frowned hard, pushing it away as she came to join the line of guests being welcomed by their hosts. Lord Barrington had upset her, she reminded herself, for he had been very rude to her when they had first spoken at the soiree last evening.

Although his letter was very well written and filled with many compliments, she considered, nodding slowly to herself as the line moved steadily forward. *Perhaps he was not displeased with me last evening but, mayhap, it was his sister.*

These thoughts lingered as she greeted Lord and Lady Folkstone, thanking them for inviting her and commenting on the loveliness of the evening as well as the beautiful decorations she had seen upon arrival. She knew precisely what to say and what was expected of her and Lord and Lady Folkstone appeared very satisfied with what she had said. Making her way into the ballroom alongside Lady Hayward, Selina held her breath and tried to push away the swirl of anxiety which swayed her stomach. The ballroom was already very busy indeed, with the musicians playing for those who had taken to the floor to dance.

"A very crowded evening, I should think," Lady Hayward remarked, as Selina nodded, trying to smile. "We shall have to be careful not to lose each other this evening, Lady Selina."

"I will do my best to always return to you immediately, should I be asked to dance," Selina replied, her heart thumping in a most uncomfortable manner. "Although there may not be any such requests!"

"Lady Selina, how wonderful to see you this evening!"

She turned hastily, recognizing one Lord Aldridge, who had evidently seen her enter the room and had made his way towards her. He was a handsome gentleman and very kind indeed, but with only the title of Viscount, Selina knew that he would never be accepted by her father as a suitable match and that, most likely, Lord Aldridge knew that also. Still, that did not prevent him from seeking out her company!

"Might I hope that I am the first to ask to peruse your dance card this evening?" Lord Aldridge asked, after quickly greeting Lady Hayward. "I must hope that I am, for I should very much like to choose the very best two dances to claim for myself!"

Selina smiled at him and handed him her dance card without hesitation, seeing Lady Hayward's knowing look and finding herself resisting the urge to laugh. After saying, only a moment before, that she was not certain that anyone would ask her to dance, she now had Lord Aldridge placing his name down for a dance!

"The cotillion," he said, handing her back the card and bowing low. "I do hope that is satisfactory?"

"You are very kind," Selina replied, accepting it back from him. "Thank you, Lord Aldridge."

The noise of someone clearing their throat caught Selina's attention and, as she turned, she was astonished to see none other than Lord Barrington approaching, a twinkle in his eye and a small smile on his lips.

"I do hope that Lord Aldridge has not stolen you for *all* of the dances left on your dance card this evening," he said, as Selina's stomach twisted with a sudden, inexplicable tension. "I should like to ask you to dance also, Lady Selina."

"Of course I have not!" Lord Aldridge replied, with a hearty chuckle. "But I will say that I am very glad indeed to have been the first to write my name down upon Lady Selina's dance card, for now I feel quite happy that I have chosen the very best of dances." He bowed again, his boyish face lighting up with good humor. "Until the cotillion, Lady Selina."

"Thank you, Lord Aldridge."

She turned back to Lord Barrington, wondering if she ought to say something about his letter to her today, only to realize that he was holding his hand out expectantly. A little embarrassed, she slipped the ribbon from her wrist and handed it to him quickly, daring a glance at Lady Hayward who was, much to her surprise, watching Lord Barrington with a rather sharp gaze.

"Thank you for your letter this afternoon, Lord Barrington," Selina found herself saying, almost tripping over her words as she hurried to speak clearly. "I was very glad to receive it."

Lord Barrington glanced up at her from under his brows, his blue eyes still bright and sending a slight tremor through Selina's frame as she caught her breath, although she could not quite understand why such a thing occurred. The intensity of his gaze made her feel as though they were melded together and it was only when he looked away that she finally managed to take in another breath.

"I am very grateful to you, as I have expressed," he said, quietly. "I should like to call upon you, Lady Selina, so that I might thank both you and Lady Hayward properly." With a smile, he looked up and handed her back her dance card, although his eyes strayed to Lady Hayward rather than lingering on her. "If such a call would be welcome."

"More than welcome, Lord Barrington," Lady Hayward replied, as Selina looked down at her dance card. "Although there is really no need. You have already thanked us both."

Lord Barrington shook his head.

"I know Lord Telford's reputation, as I am sure you do also, Lady Hayward," he answered, as Selina realized with a start that he had written his name for the supper dance. "My sister was foolish. There could have been a great deal of difficulty caused and I – I would like to express my thanks most sincerely." Selina looked up at him just as he returned his gaze to her. "I do hope you have no objections, Lady Selina?" he asked, making her wonder if he spoke of his desire to call upon her or the dances he had chosen. "I am, of course, entirely dependent upon your agreement."

"Of course not, Lord Barrington," she replied quickly, praying that the warmth she felt in her cheeks would soon dissipate. "I have no objections whatsoever. Thank you for your consideration."

The smile on his face sent another streak of warmth into her face but Selina managed to keep his gaze and did not look away, despite her blushes.

"Very good," he said, bowing low. "Until our dance, Lady Selina."

She smiled back at him despite the trembling in her soul, confused as to why she had such a strong reaction towards him, when only last evening, she had thought him both rude and easily displeased.

"Well, I do not think you need fear that your dance card will remain empty this evening, Lady Selina!" Lady Hayward remarked, as Selina managed to laugh, aware of just how hot her cheeks were. "You have at least two dances filled within only a few minutes!" She smiled at her. "What dance did Lord Barrington choose?"

Selina did not reply but instead handed her chaperone the card, watching for her reaction. Lady Hayward did not disappoint. Her brows rose, her eyes widened and she looked back at Selina with a somewhat astonished expression.

"The supper dance? And a second dance as well!" she remarked, as Selina nodded. "My goodness, Lady

Selina. It appears that you may have something of an admirer in Lord Barrington."

"I am sure that he is only doing so by way of thanks for what we did for Lady Amelia," Selina replied, hastily. "I do not think there can be anything more meant by it."

Lady Hayward considered this for a moment, then shrugged.

"We shall have to wait and see!" she declared, as Selina took back her dance card. "But do allow yourself to consider Lord Barrington, Lady Selina. He is an Earl and a very respectable one at that, with an excellent fortune and more than able to keep you very contented indeed for the rest of your days. I am sure that your father would agree."

Finding herself laughing suddenly, Selina held up both hands, palms out towards Lady Hayward.

"Pray, do not think so quickly of what might be, Lady Hayward!" she exclaimed, as Lady Hayward looked surprised and then began to laugh also. "I do not even know Lord Barrington as yet, for we are barely acquainted! And I remind you that you have been eagerly encouraging me to consider my heart, should the opportunity for courtship or the like present itself."

Lady Hayward lifted one eyebrow.

"Indeed, I have," she agreed, her eyes holding something that Selina could not quite make out. "I have always encouraged you to consider what you might feel when it comes to the gentlemen of London and to those who might pay you a little more attention. However, I do not believe that there is not even a flicker of interest within your heart when it comes to Lord Barrington."

Shock filled Selina's heart as she looked back at her companion, flushing with embarrassment. She had thought that such emotions, such confusion had been easily hidden, that she had managed to keep any inflection from her voice every time she had spoken of him – but evidently, she had failed in doing so.

"It is only this evening that I have noticed it," Lady Hayward continued, reaching out to press Selina's arm. "It is not something that you need to be ashamed of, Lady Selina, and it may very well prove to be nothing of importance, for once you are a little better acquainted with Lord Barrington, you might find him to be very dull indeed, or to have a temper that you dislike intensely. But, for the moment, do not hide away what you feel from yourself. Enjoy the dances with Lord Barrington and do what you can to converse with him." Her smile widened whilst Selina's sense of confusion and embarrassment only grew. "There is nothing more you need do at present."

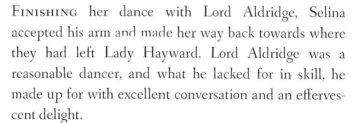

Finishing her dance with Lord Aldridge, Selina accepted his arm and made her way back towards where they had left Lady Hayward. Lord Aldridge was a reasonable dancer, and what he lacked for in skill, he made up for with excellent conversation and an effervescent delight.

"I do not see Lady Hayward," Lord Aldridge murmured, as they made their way back towards those who waited by the side of the dance floor. "Where might she have gone?"

"It is a very busy evening," Selina replied, a little embarrassed that she would have to linger with Lord Aldridge a little longer. "She might well have become lost in the crowd. I am sure I will be able to find her."

Lord Aldridge let out a rumble of laughter.

"Do not think that you are in any way importuning me, Lady Selina," he said, gallantly. "I am very glad to have you by my side a little longer."

Selina smiled but managed to extract her arm from his, not wanting anyone to see them still walking so and beginning to whisper about them.

"I am certain she is nearby," she said, knowing that Lady Hayward would, most likely, be looking for her just as much as Selina was searching for her. "There are very many guests here this evening!"

Lord Aldridge chuckled.

"Just as Lord Folkstone likes it," he replied, clearly not in any hurry to step away from her. "Shall we take a turn about the room, Lady Selina?"

Seeing that there was very little option for her to do anything but that, Selina acquiesced and together, they walked through the crowd, searching for Lady Hayward.

"Mayhap she has stepped outside?" Lord Aldridge suggested, although a cold hand of fright clasped at Selina's heart as they passed the open doors that led to the garden. "If you would not be noticed and if it would not inconvenience you, Lady Selina, might I suggest that you wait here for my return? I shall search for Lady Hayward for a few minutes and return to you."

Selina let out a long breath of relief, glad that Lord Aldridge did not intend to pull her out into the darkness. It seemed that he was a gentleman in every respect.

"I am sure I can wait here," Selina replied, knowing that the situation was rather awkward and that, whilst she ought to linger with someone, it was best to find Lady Hayward as soon as they could. There seemed very little possibility that Lady Hayward had stepped out of doors for any reason but given that Selina could not see her anywhere else, Selina had no other choice but to permit Lord Aldridge to take a few moments to look.

"There is a seat to your left," he said, gesturing towards it. "I will be only a few moments."

Selina nodded and made her way there, glad that she would be out of sight of most of the other guests. Sitting down quickly, she passed one hand over her eyes and drew in a long breath, stifling any panic that tried to capture her heart. Lady Hayward would be present somewhere. And when she found her, Selina was certain there would be a reasonable and understandable explanation.

"What are you *doing*?"

Her heart began to thump furiously as, out of the corner of her eye, she saw a gentleman approach a lady and take her by the elbow. Remaining precisely where she was and making certain not to lift her gaze to the gentleman in question, Selina caught her breath as she realized it was none other than Lady Amelia. The lady she had been speaking with did not appear to notice what had taken place, and as Selina remained seated, uncertain as to what she ought to do, the gentleman pulled Lady

Amelia away from her companions and walked past
Selina. Turning her head, Selina watched as he led Lady
Amelia to the door – although quite where it led, Selina
did not know.

Her heart turned over in her chest. She looked back
at the lady that had been in conversation with Lady
Amelia and was astonished to find that she had not even
seemed to notice the lady's absence. Instead, she was
busy conversing with another, laughing and smiling as
though nothing was wrong.

What do I do?

With tension running through her veins, Selina
returned her gaze to Lady Amelia and the gentleman. He
was encouraging her to go through the door with him and
Selina wanted desperately to go directly towards her and
demand that she return with her at once. But her courage
failed her. With bated breath, she watched Lady Amelia
sigh, tilt her head and look straight up into the gentleman's eyes, only to shake her head sorrowfully. The
gentleman placed one hand on Lady Amelia's shoulder
and ran his fingers down her arm – but Lady Amelia
shook her head and, much to Selina's relief, stepped back.
Within a few moments, she had walked away from him,
her head held high and a slight color to her cheeks.

Selina let out a breath of relief. Relief which was
short lived, disrupted by an all too close voice.

"You did not succeed then."

Jerking her head back around – and grateful that her
chair was hidden amongst the shadows of the room,
Selina saw none other than Lord Telford coming to speak
to the first gentleman, who still had his back to her.

"I did not succeed," the first replied, darkly. "It seems she is not as eager as you had expected."

Lord Telford snorted. "I hardly believe that to be true," he said, with a smug smile. "It may be that she simply disliked your attentions! I think, come the next time, *I* should be the one to... encourage the lady."

The first gentleman muttered something indistinguishable and Selina closed her eyes and turned her head away, still listening intently but wanting to give no impression whatsoever that she was watching them.

"We will have our funds," she heard Lord Telford state, with absolute certainty ringing through his voice. "I had Lord Barrington in my sights, ready to grasp him by the arm and practically drag him to where you were with Lady Amelia, but it seems that we shall have to change places come the next opportunity."

"But I do not know Lord Barrington."

"Then I suggest you find a way to make your introductions," Lord Telford stated, angrily. "Now, if you will excuse me, I intend to go and find the very best brandy and allow myself a few minutes to revel in my disappointment."

Selina's breathing was ragged, such was her shock. She had overheard something of a plot, it seemed, something that would bring Lord Barrington *and* Lady Amelia a good deal of pain. Her head began to spin as she put one hand to her mouth, realizing just what this meant.

But will Lady Amelia give in to Lord Telford's advances?

The question in her mind did not wait long for an answer. She knew very well that Lord Barrington would have given his sister a stern talking to and that, quite certainly, Lady Amelia knew precisely what was expected of her. However, Selina also knew how Lady Amelia had behaved in the past, when it came to Lord Telford. There was a chance that the lady would refuse – but if she did so again for what would be the second time, Selina feared that Lord Telford might force her to go as he expected.

And Lord Barrington would have to witness what followed.

No doubt Lord Telford and the other gentleman intended to gain money from Lord Barrington by promising to remain silent. It was all truly disastrous and Selina knew she needed to speak to Lord Telford at once.

"Ah, there you are!"

An older lady came towards her, with Lord Aldridge just behind her.

"I have been looking everywhere for you!" the lady exclaimed, just as Lord Aldridge joined them. "Lady Hayward has had something of an accident. She will be waiting for you in the carriage."

Alarm seared Selina's heart. "She is injured?"

"A slight accident, as I have said," the older lady replied, although, much to Selina's dismay, she did not give any further details. Glancing at the gentleman and clearly recognizing him, the lady gestured to him swiftly. "Come now. You also, if you wish, Lord Aldridge. Accompany the lady."

Lord Aldridge nodded and offered Selina his arm, which she took at once, feeling a little lightheaded as she walked alongside him.

"As I have said, she is waiting for you in the carriage," the lady said, encouragingly. "A twisted ankle, that is all it is, I am sure. She will be quite well in a very short time indeed."

Selina nodded but said nothing, her thoughts drifting between concern for Lady Hayward and worry over Lady Amelia and Lord Barrington. She would have to write to Lord Barrington in the morning, she determined, for he had to know of what she had overheard just as soon as was possible. To keep it to herself would not only be wrong but entirely unthinkable.

"I am sure all will be well," Lord Aldridge murmured, as they made their way through the crowd towards the door that would lead them out of the ballroom. "No need to fret."

Selina gave him a tight smile.

"I hope it will be, Lord Aldridge," she murmured, throwing one last glance over her shoulder as though she might be able to see Lord Barrington. But the ballroom was too crowded and with a heavy sigh, Selina turned away from them all and made her way through the door.

CHAPTER SIX

Charles stepped into the drawing room to what was a rather tense scene. His mother was standing, her hands on her hips, glaring at her daughter. Lady Amelia was sitting demurely in a chair, looking back at her with a calm if not somewhat supercilious expression, which Charles knew would only make his mother all the more irritated.

"Is something wrong, Mama?" he asked, closing the door behind him so that none of the staff would hear him speak. "You appear a little upset."

Lady Barrington shook her head and let her hands drop to her sides.

"You speak to your sister, Barrington," she said, wearily. "I did not want to inform you of this but I was told by Lady Fitzherbert last evening that your sister stepped away from Lady Pembrokeshire for a few minutes."

Charles' heart twisted in his chest.

"I beg your pardon?" he asked, looking towards his

sister who, to his frustration, merely gazed back at him without any trace of embarrassment or shame. "What is the meaning of this, Amelia?"

Lady Amelia let out a long sigh, as though she was tired of them both.

"I did nothing of the sort," she said. "A gentleman I am acquainted with spoke to me quietly and I returned the conversation before making my way back to Lady Pembrokeshire."

Closing his eyes, Charles drew in a deep breath.

"You returned to Lady Pembrokeshire?" he repeated, as the small, flickering smile faded from Lady Amelia's face. "What do you mean, 'returned'?"

"I – I..." She stopped for a moment, now appearing a little flustered as she tried to speak clearly. "It is not as though I quit the room or walked far from her, Barrington! I did nothing of the sort! It was only a step or two away from Lady Pembrokeshire's side and she herself did not notice nor complain. I always remained in her view and –"

"And what is the name of the gentleman?" Charles interrupted, his voice loud and determined. "You will tell me at once, Amelia!"

She rose from her chair, her hands balling into fists by her side.

"I shall not," she stated, firmly. "Else, no doubt, you will demand that I never be in his company again. There was nothing wrong with my behavior nor my conduct, Barrington. You take the word of someone you are not very well acquainted with over that of my own! That is entirely unfair!"

"I trust Lady Fitzherbert!" Charles' mother protested loudly, but Charles held up one hand, asking her to be quiet for the moment.

"Amelia, there should be not even a *hint* of impropriety from you," he stated, as his sister scowled and looked away. "I do not know what you were doing precisely last evening but if you were seen talking to a gentleman in a secluded fashion, then that is not at all appropriate – and you must know that!"

"I will return you to the estate if you do any such thing again," Lady Barrington interrupted, taking a step closer to her daughter. "I have heard your brother reprimand you severely already, Amelia, and for him to continue to tolerate your behavior speaks of a greater patience than I have!" She waggled one finger at her, her irritation and upset already evident. "This is your only warning, Amelia. There can be *nothing* more."

Lady Amelia dropped her head and, after a moment, nodded. Charles shook his head, running one hand over his eyes and wondering if he should be taking Amelia to this evening's assembly. It was certainly going to be an excellent evening but there would be a great many people present and he feared that Amelia might choose to behave in a fashion that verged on impropriety, given what she had done last evening.

"I will do as you say," Lady Amelia said, her voice low with no trace of a smile on her face. "I did not mean to upset you both."

Charles did not know whether to believe this or not but after stating one more time, very clearly, that there would be no further opportunities to prove herself should she continue along this path, he gestured to his mother and the three of them made their way to the door.

"My Lord?"

The butler was waiting for him.

"Might I remind you, my Lord, that you have still urgent correspondence?"

Charles hesitated, his mother and sister going on ahead of him. He had slept for a longer time than usual that morning and thereafter had spent the afternoon in town and accompanying his sister during her walk in Hyde Park for the fashionable hour.

"Might you remind me who it was from?" he asked, as Jamison inclined his head.

"A Lady Selina, if I recall correctly," came the reply. "The fellow who brought it stated that the lady begged you to open it at once."

"Do hurry up, Barrington!"

The call of his mother sent a slight wave of frustration through Charles but he kept his expression entirely blank.

"I am sure I will see Lady Selina this evening," he said, with a small shrug. "I will speak to her of her letter and apologize for my lack of response."

The butler nodded, wished him a pleasant evening and withdrew, although Charles' frown remained as he made his way to the front of the house, ready to step out into the carriage. Whatever had Lady Selina written that was of such great importance? Part of him wanted to hurry back to his study, to find the letter and read it so that, at the very least, he would know what it was that she had said before he saw her again that evening, but he knew he could not do so, not when his mother and sister were waiting.

"Do not forget what was said, Amelia," Charles warned, as the carriage pulled away. "Nothing will be tolerated. One foolish choice and we shall make our way back to the estate where you will spend the rest of spring and all of the summer regretting your ridiculous decisions. Am I quite clear?"

There was silence for a moment or two and then, after a moment, Lady Amelia sniffed and murmured that she understood. Satisfied, Charles leaned back against the squabs and closed his eyes, his thoughts returning to Lady Selina.

She was, he had to admit, a very lovely young lady. She bore no ill will, it seemed, for even though his sister had changed her manner towards Lady Selina upon discovering she was the daughter of a Duke – a change that he was certain Lady Selina herself had noticed – the lady was gracious enough to continue a conversation with his sister. And then, when Amelia had turned towards her friend without even ending her conversation properly with Lady Selina, Charles had felt such an embarrassment rise within him that he had wanted to apologize, only to find *himself* distracted in a very similar fashion!

Being quite certain that the lady would no longer wish to remain in their acquaintance, he had been astonished to see her standing with Lady Amelia and Miss Newington only a short time later. His admiration for her had grown all the more as he had realized what she had done, and since that moment, he had found himself thinking very well of her indeed. Certainly, she appeared to be a little quiet and reserved, and on some occasions, her conversation was a little lacking, but there was a heart of great compassion and consideration within her, he was sure of it. She was, he considered, the sort of young lady he wished might become a very close acquaintance of his sister, merely so that she might choose to behave a little better, but given that Lady Amelia and Lady Selina were of such different characters, he doubted such a thing would ever occur.

His thoughts drifted back towards the letter that Lady Selina had sent to him, wondering again at its urgency. What had she written that demanded his immediate attention? Sighing, he shook his head to himself and pinched the bridge of his nose as though to rid himself of an irritation. Whatever it was, he would find Lady Selina that very evening and apologize to her for his lack of time in reading the letter. No doubt she would be able to inform him of its contents this evening. Charles just had to hope he was not too late in learning of it.

"Have you seen Lady Selina this evening?" Lord Banfield's eyebrows rose with such swiftness that Charles wanted to laugh aloud. "I seek her only to ask about a letter she sent to me," he continued, before Banfield could even begin to exclaim over Charles' request. "And not for any other reason, I assure you."

The surprise and evident delight that had been beginning to spread across Banfield's face immediately fell away.

"I see," he muttered, as though he was a little disappointed. "And I thought that you were going to be in search of her for some other purpose!"

Charles grinned.

"I am very well aware of that," he replied, as Banfield sighed heavily. "No, it is only that she wrote to me this afternoon – an urgent letter, by my butler's account – and I did not have the opportunity to read it."

"An urgent letter?" Banfield replied, now looking a little surprised. "And you have no knowledge of what might be contained within it?"

"None," Charles replied, with a shake of his head. "I do feel a little embarrassed that I did not have time to read it, and wanted to speak to her this evening, not only to apologize, but to ask her what was contained within it."

"I do not think that you will find her here this evening," Banfield replied, with a small frown. "I did hear that Lady Hayward, her chaperone, had encountered something of an accident."

A frown caught Charles' brow.

"Oh?"

"It was at last evening's ball," Banfield explained. "I do not know the particulars, but I did hear Lord Aldridge say that he had been required to accompany Lady Selina to the carriage, where Lady Hayward was waiting. Apparently, some oaf had knocked into her – having been somewhat inebriated, I believe – and she stumbled and injured her ankle."

"And therefore, you would not expect her to be present this evening," Charles finished, a little frustrated.

"Well, I can do nothing else but return home and read this letter, then!"

Banfield shrugged.

"I am sure that, had it been of *great* urgency, she would have written to you again, or called upon you in person," he said, in a clear attempt to quieten Charles' frustration. "You can read it the moment you return home from this evening."

Nodding, Charles let out a long breath, passing one hand over his eyes.

"Indeed," he agreed, heavily. "I confess I have had a good deal on my mind of late. My sister is, yet again –"

"Let me guess," Banfield interrupted, with a small smile. "She has not done as you asked?"

Finding nothing to laugh about, Charles grimaced.

"My mother, at least, is being a good deal more supportive of my actions, but it seems that Amelia is refusing to do *precisely* as she is told." He shook his head. "I believe that last evening, she stepped away from her companion in order to talk to another gentleman in private."

Banfield frowned, the smile fading away.

"I see."

"This evening, I fully expect her to stay directly by my mother's side, however," Charles continued, with a shake of his head. "She did attempt to defend her behavior last evening but I have warned her that there shall not be even a hint of impropriety this evening, else she shall be returned to the estate without hesitation!"

Tilting his head, Banfield considered for a moment.

"Mayhap I could assist you a little, should you wish

it?" he asked, as Charles frowned. "I could make certain to dance with Lady Amelia at each ball, make sure to converse with her at every soiree and the like?"

"That is very generous of you, Banfield," Charles replied, a little surprised at the gentleman's suggestion. "But there is no need, unless you truly wish to do so. I know that you are, yourself, seeking a bride."

Banfield shrugged.

"It would not be overly difficult," he replied, with a smile. "Besides which, it would allow *you* opportunity to converse with someone such as Lady Selina, should you wish it! And I do not mind dancing and conversing with a beautiful young lady such as Lady Amelia!"

Not wishing to remind Banfield that he had his mother to take over supervision of Lady Amelia whenever he wished, Charles gave his friend a broad smile.

"Then I will accept your offer," he answered, appreciating his friend's consideration. "She is with my mother at present. I think that..."

He trailed off, suddenly spying his mother and noting with concern that his sister was not with her. His heart quickened as he made his way towards her, Lord Banfield following after him. He tried to convince himself that there was nothing to be concerned about – there was dancing this evening after all, and his sister was, most likely, standing up with someone. Surely, she would not be as foolish as to behave improperly now!

"Barrington." His mother smiled brightly as they drew near, greeting Lord Banfield with the same warm smile she had given to Charles. "Are you quite all right?"

Glancing at the lady who his mother had been talking

with, only to see her turn away to speak with another, Charles let out a long breath.

"Amelia," he said, as his mother's eyes flared wide. "Where is she?"

Lady Barrington reached out and pressed his arm.

"She is dancing," she said, quietly. "My dear son, you are very good to be so concerned about your sister and, believe me, I quite understand your concern, but the gentleman she was with was most proper and promised to return her the moment the dance came to an end."

Charles' heart slammed hard into his chest as he looked up, suddenly realizing that there was no longer any music. He looked back at his mother, his mouth pulling into a grim line.

"Then, where is she?"

Silence grew between Charles and his mother as they looked all about them, with Lord Banfield's brow furrowing hard where he stood beside them. The couples who had been dancing were now moving away, the ladies being returned to their mothers or companions, and the gentlemen bowing in evident gratitude. However, of Lady Amelia and her gentleman, there was no sign.

"This gentleman," Charles said, firmly, looking towards his mother and seeing the paleness in her cheeks. "What was his name?"

"I – I have been introduced to him before," his mother replied, weakly. "Amelia has been also. They have danced before. They –"

"His name, mother."

Lady Barrington took in a long breath and closed her eyes, evidently steadying herself.

"It is Lord Havers," she said, as Charles held his gaze fixed to her own, seeing how her eyes fluttered open. "As I have said, Barrington, he is not a new acquaintance."

Charles grimaced.

"Which might make things all the worse," he growled, looking to Banfield. "Are you acquainted with the gentleman? I do not think I –"

"Lord Barrington?"

Turning sharply, Charles looked at the gentleman who had approached him, his heart still filled with anger towards his sister and dread at what he might discover.

"Yes?"

It was none other than Lord Telford. Charles' expression darkened all the more, for he thought very little of the gentleman and, given what had occurred recently with his sister, he was not at all inclined to engage with the gentleman in any way.

"I do not mean to speak out of turn, Lord Barrington," Lord Telford began, taking a small step closer and lowering his voice so that even Lady Barrington struggled to hear what was being said. "But I am certain that I observed your sister being led out of doors by a gentleman. I am aware that I have no right to criticize given my own behavior of late, but it is your sister that I think of."

Sucking in a breath, Charles felt his chest tighten.

"Indeed," he said, a trifle coldly. "And you thought to come and inform me of this, rather than gossip about it?"

Lord Telford nodded and Charles felt a slight stab of guilt press against his heart.

"Then you have not spoken to anyone else of this?"

"I have not," Lord Telford replied, earnestly. "Pray,

might you attend with me? I will show you where she has gone at once."

Charles had no other choice but to agree.

"Might you stay with my mother?" he asked Lord Banfield, reaching out to press his mother's hand. "I will return very soon. And hopefully with Amelia."

Lord Banfield nodded, whilst Charles' mother made to say something, only to press her hand to her mouth. Charles stepped away from them, following Lord Telford, and wondering at what he might discover. His heart was pounding furiously, his anger growing with every step. He had *warned* Amelia, had he not? He had made it quite clear that she was not to do anything that might damage her reputation – and yet she had done precisely that. The sense of disappointment which enveloped him was utterly overwhelming. He had never wanted to force his sister into matrimony, had always wanted to give her the opportunity to find a suitable match herself, but if she intended to continue in this vein, then what choice did he have?

Unless I am too late already.

His brow furrowed and he shook his head as Lord Telford took him the open doors which led outside. There were only a few lanterns, meaning that he was enveloped in near darkness almost at once.

"I am sure that I saw them turn this way," Lord Telford murmured, his voice a good deal quieter than before. "If we might –"

Stopping dead, he held up one hand, as though to silence any response that might come from Charles. For a moment, Charles heard nothing, only for a quiet voice to float towards him.

"I have asked you to unhand me!"

Amelia.

Closing his eyes, Charles took in a long breath and then stepped forward, pushing past Lord Telford and stepping further into the growing darkness.

"Come now, Lady Amelia!" he heard a gentleman say. "There is no need for any reluctance!"

"Unhand me!"

Charles frowned. There was a tremor in his sister's voice which spoke of fear and upset, rather than any sort of delight. She was not laughing nor teasing the gentleman in question but, it seemed, was asking him to leave her alone. The gentleman was refusing.

It is a little late to have regret now, Charles thought to himself grimly, finally coming across the two figures in the darkness.

"Amelia!"

The gentleman released Amelia's arm and stepped back, whilst Amelia herself let out first a gasp, and then a cry of relief, before flinging herself into Charles' arms.

Charles stiffened.

"An explanation, if you please," he said, only for the gentleman to laugh harshly and then quickly step away from them both in the darkness, leaving Charles all the more furious. Grasping Amelia's shoulders, he bent his head and looked at her, trying to make out her features in the gloom. "You must understand the consequences of this, Amelia," he said, forcing himself to keep his temper. "We are leaving at once."

To his very great surprise, Amelia did not let him go. She did not step back and flounce away, nor try to defend herself. Instead, she began to sob against his shoulder, her whole body shaking.

"Amelia," he said again, firmly. "That is enough. You must –"

"He would not let me go!" she cried, lifting her head to look up at him as Charles pulled his handkerchief from his pocket and handed it to her. She fumbled for a moment but took it, wiping her eyes and sniffing wretchedly. "I am telling you the truth, Barrington," she continued, a little more calmly, her voice still shaking. "He would not let me go and I could not scream for fear of causing such a disturbance that you might be all the more ashamed of me."

"Home," he gritted out, his whole body burning with an anger that he knew he could not express. "At once, Amelia."

Her shoulders slumped, her head dropping low.

"Of course, you do not believe me," she said softly. "I speak nothing but lies to you, is that not so?"

Charles said nothing, for fear that he might explode with fury. Instead, he grasped her shoulder and turned her bodily towards the door.

"Charles," Amelia whimpered, although she did move forward slowly. "Please, I –"

"Control yourself, Amelia," he retorted, relieved beyond measure that none of the other guests had seen Amelia. "We will go back inside, find Mama, and then make our way to the carriage. And we will speak of this again in the morning. Plans will be made and you *will* do as I tell you."

His sister lapsed into silence, although Charles could still hear her sniffing now and again. His heart was hardened towards her suffering, believing that everything she had said and done was entirely her own fault. She would not be able to escape from this situation now. It was much too serious and Charles knew the consequences had to be severe.

"Amelia!"

The way his mother reached for her daughter made it all too apparent that she had been anxious about her and thus, Charles gave her a small shake of his head.

"You have discovered her, then," Lord Banfield said, quietly, as Amelia dropped her head, lifting Charles' handkerchief to her eyes. "Lord Telford returned to the room shortly after you both stepped outside."

Quickly directing his mother to take Amelia to the carriage, Charles waited until they had left his side before allowing himself to reply.

"It appears I owe Lord Telford a great deal of thanks," he said, discovering that his hands were now clenched tightly into fists, his nails digging into the soft skin of his palms. "And he is a gentleman I never expected to have to thank."

Banfield nodded, his expression serious.

"What will you do?"

"There is only one thing I can do," Charles replied, heavily. "Return her to my estate and seek a suitable gentleman on her behalf. She has disgraced herself and come very close to disgracing the family name also."

With a shake of his head, Banfield let out a long breath.

"I wish you success with whatever you discuss come the morrow," he said, kindly. "Do inform me as to whether or not you yourself will accompany her or if you will remain in London."

Charles gave his friend a tight smile.

"I will," he promised, his heart sinking heavily in his chest. "Thank you, Banfield."

CHAPTER SEVEN

Selina bit her lip as she began to pace up and down in front of the mantlepiece. Lord Barrington had not replied to her letter, as she had begged him to do, so that she might know he was aware of the danger. Last evening, had Lady Hayward not injured herself the night before, they would have attended the ball but, given her chaperone's injury, Selina had been forced to remain at home.

Thus far, she had heard nothing about the ball itself which, she hoped, meant that there was nothing of particular concern. However, if what she had overheard the previous evening was correct, then it meant that Lord Barrington was *supposed* to have discovered his sister in a certain situation, and that situation be kept as quiet as possible at the time. Lord Barrington would soon be approached, she was sure of it, if he had not been already, and told what payment was expected from him, in order to keep the gentlemen in question quiet about what Lady Amelia had supposedly done.

"Lady Hayward, my Lady."

Selina started violently at the footman's announcement, and turned to see Lady Hayward limping into the room, although the limp itself was not particularly pronounced.

"Lady Hayward," she breathed, hurrying forward so that she might offer the lady some assistance, but her chaperone laughed and shook her head, clearly determined to make her way to the chair herself.

"I am not about to linger at home and wait for my ankle to recover itself," she said, firmly. "I cannot abide sitting around and doing nothing whatsoever!"

Selina waited until the lady sat down before speaking, her eyes filled with anxiety.

"But you are unwell still," she said, as Lady Hayward smiled back at her. "You should be resting."

"So my sons have been telling me, but I shall not listen to them," Lady Hayward replied, firmly. "I have only just –"

Before she could speak, the door opened again and, much to Selina's surprise, her father stepped into the room. He did not so much as glance towards Selina herself, but rather looked towards Lady Hayward.

"Lady Hayward," he said, with a quick bow of his head. "I was informed that you had come to call on Selina. I thought to see how you fared." A small frown flickered across his brow. "The butler mentioned that you were not walking as freely as one might have hoped."

Selina, a little surprised that her father had decided to emerge from his study simply to speak to Lady Hayward and make certain that she was well, watched the concern flicker across the Duke's expression with interest. Lady Hayward smiled warmly at him, her blue eyes meeting his.

"I am much recovered, Your Grace," she replied, evidently grateful for his concern. "My ankle is still a little painful, certainly, but it is not something that troubles me a great deal." She glanced back at Selina. "Besides which, I knew that Lady Selina would be worrying about me and so I thought it best to visit just as soon as I could."

"Well, I am glad to see you recovering," the Duke replied, as Selina dropped into a chair, wisely choosing to remain quite silent.

She listened as the Duke and her chaperone talked of a few other matters – mostly about the gentleman who had caused Lady Hayward's accident in the first place and whether or not he was even *aware* of what he had done – before, finally, the Duke chose to take his leave.

Selina rose with him and rang the bell for tea, smiling at her father as he looked towards her.

"You will be glad to have Lady Hayward back with you, I know," the Duke said kindly, as Selina nodded. "It is good to see you smile, Selina."

"Thank you, Father."

She waited until her father had left the room before letting out a long, pained sigh, rubbing one hand across her forehead and feeling a knot of tension tighten her stomach.

"Lady Selina?" Lady Hayward asked, as Selina looked back at her, having no urge to resume her seat. "Is something wrong?"

Selina, who was still a little intrigued by her father's obvious concern for Lady Hayward, chose *not* to speak of that particular thing but instead, realized that she could, in fact, share with Lady Hayward what she had overheard some two nights ago. There had not been an opportunity to do so before, given what had happened to Lady Hayward and her ankle, but now, perhaps, was the right time.

"There has been a matter weighing heavily upon my mind these last two days," she began, starting once more to pace the length of the room as her skirts swished gently. "It is to do with Lord Barrington." Lady Hayward's eyes flickered but she said nothing, clearly choosing to remain silent as Selina spoke. "When you had your accident, I was with Lord Aldridge, as you know," Selina continued, forced to stop for a few moments as the maid brought in the tea tray and set it down on a side table near Lady Hayward.

"Shall I pour?" Lady Hayward asked, as Selina nodded. "I can tell that you have a great deal on your mind."

"Please do," Selina murmured. "Whilst we were searching for you, I overheard something. Something dreadful."

Quickly, she explained to Lady Hayward what Lord Telford had said, frustrated that she did not know the name of the second gentleman.

"Goodness!" Lady Hayward exclaimed, the tea now steaming gently in the two china teacups. "And did you inform Lord Barrington of..." She trailed off, a look of understanding coming into her eyes. "Of course, you could not call upon him, given my inability to be present with you. And last evening, you remained at home."

"I had no wish to step outside into society, I assure you," Selina replied, her fingers twisting together as she kept her hands in front of her, still pacing up and down the room. "After what I overheard, the only thing I wished for was to inform Lord Barrington of the plans that were being made for both himself and Lady Amelia. Unfortunately," she continued, with a shake of her head, "I am not certain that he read the letter I sent him, despite my request that he do so with the greatest urgency."

Lady Hayward sighed with evident frustration and waved Selina into a chair. Feeling a little less tense, now that she had told Lady Hayward everything, Selina did as she was instructed and sat down, reaching for her teacup and saucer so that she might take a sip.

"It may be that Lord Barrington did *not* read your letter," Lady Hayward said softly, as Selina closed her eyes. "I have heard no gossip from last evening, but I suppose that is to be expected, given what Lord Telford intends."

"Precisely," Selina replied, reaching for a honey cake. "But if Lord Barrington has *still* not read my letter – for I did beg him to inform me that he had done so, in order for my own mind to be at ease – then it means that something dreadful might have occurred last evening, and he will think that it is solely Lady Amelia's doing."

Lady Hayward nodded, but remained silent. Sipping her tea, she waited for a few minutes before she spoke again.

"Then there is only one course of action open to us," she said eventually, as Selina finished the last of her tea. "We must make our way to Lord Barrington's townhouse and demand that he speak with you."

Selina's eyes flared as her heart immediately began to quicken.

"But I –"

"I know there is a lack of confidence within your heart, Lady Selina," Lady Hayward continued, before Selina could finish speaking. "I know that there is a part of you which wants to retreat from society all the more, which wants to make certain that there is nothing required of you save for having written this letter, but you must be a little bolder now."

Selina swallowed hard and reached to set her teacup down.

"But surely I need not *call* upon him," she said, emphatically. "I am certain that he is in a dreadful state already, and will not be grateful for my presence."

"I believe that Lord Barrington will be very grateful for your arrival, once you have explained all!" Lady Hayward exclaimed, a fresh light sparkling in her eyes. "Have a little more courage, my dear. Lord Barrington may, at first, state that he is not receiving calls at present, but you will be required to demand it, to force it, if you must. Do you think that you can do such a thing?"

Selina wanted to shake her head, wanted to say that no, she could not, but the challenge in Lady Hayward's eyes gave her pause. If she went to Lord Barrington's townhouse, if she insisted on telling him all that she knew, then he would have no choice but to listen, and

Lady Amelia's relationship with her brother might be saved. If she said nothing, if she waited at home and prayed that her letter would finally be opened and read, then there was no promise that Lord Barrington would ever realize the truth of what was occurring. He might receive the request for funds to ensure the gentlemen to remain quiet about the matter, might be willing to pay it and would never know the truth – that his sister had done nothing wrong.

Was that a risk she wished to take?

"Very well, Lady Hayward," she said, after a few moments of silence. "Very well. But only if you feel that you are able to do so."

Lady Hayward chuckled, her eyes dancing.

"I am more than determined to attend, regardless of my ankle," she said, as Selina gave her a wan smile. "Come then, Lady Selina. Let us go."

STANDING in the doorway of Lord Barrington's townhouse, Selina drew in a long, shuddering breath and forced herself to remain strong.

"I am aware that your master has said that he is unable to see us at present," she said, wishing that Lady Hayward would speak up so that she did not have to do so. "But I must insist. It is a matter of great urgency."

The butler looked back at her, his brows low over his eyes.

"My Lady, I beg your understanding. The master is –"

"Please, return to Lord Barrington," Selina continued, her heart pounding furiously. "Tell him that what I have to say is relevant to his current situation."

Her mouth went dry as she finished speaking, knowing full well that what she had just said might mean nothing whatsoever to Lord Barrington, if all was well. Lady Amelia might be quite all right, Lord Telford might not have chosen to act and Lord Barrington might have another reason for being unable to see her.

But as she watched the butler's face, she saw something jump into his eyes, although the rest of his expression remained exactly the same.

"Very well, my Lady," he murmured, inclining his head and turning away from her, leaving Selina praying silently that what she had just seen meant something of importance.

"You spoke well," Lady Hayward murmured, as Selina closed her eyes and tried to drag a little more strength into her heart. "The butler knows that what you have to speak of is of great importance. I believe that what you overheard has already come to pass, Lady Selina."

Selina nodded and opened her eyes.

"I do hope that Lord Barrington will listen," she said, softly. "There is nothing more I can say if he refuses again."

Lady Hayward laughed softly.

"Oh, but there is!" she replied, as Selina looked back at her in surprise. "Remaining steadfast and determined means that, on occasion, one might have to behave in a manner that is both embarrassing and almost a little rude! You could state that you will not leave this house until you speak with Lord Barrington, for example." Her eyes twinkled and a smile spread across her face. "I am quite certain that no footman nor butler would be willing to place a hand upon you, my dear. Therefore, you would, in the end, be met by Lord Barrington and have the conversation you so eagerly desire."

"I do not think I could do such a thing," Selina replied, doubtfully. "I do not have the strength of character."

Lady Hayward snorted in a most unladylike fashion.

"Of course you do!" she exclaimed, as Selina shook her head. "It is within you, my dear. You have found a little of it already, given what you are doing and what you have said." She smiled at Selina, who felt herself almost sick with nervousness. "You might surprise yourself with what you are able to do when you wish it."

The sound of footsteps prevented Selina from responding, and she looked back towards the butler as he came towards them. His face held the same muted expression as he once more inclined his head towards them.

"If you would follow me," he said, gravely, as Selina's heart leapt wildly in her chest. "The master will see you now, although he begs that your visit be kept to only a few minutes."

This was a little surprising to hear from a butler, although Selina held her tongue and said nothing in response. Lord Barrington, she was sure, would be willing to have her in his home for a little longer once he realized what she knew. All that mattered now was to make certain that he knew everything that she herself had learned.

Stepping into Lord Barrington's drawing room, Selina saw Lord Barrington rise from a chair near the unlit fireplace. The room was a little cold – for the day was not particularly warm – and from the paleness of Lord Barrington's cheeks, Selina wondered if there ought to be a little warmth brought into the room for his sake.

"Lady Selina," Lord Barrington muttered, bowing quickly. "Lady Hayward." His brow furrowed as he took in Lady Hayward's limp. "You are injured!"

"I am quite all right," Lady Hayward replied, sitting down quickly. "It is nothing."

Selina waited until Lord Barrington asked her to be seated before she too sat down, looking at the gentleman and seeing the anxiety written all over his face. His blue eyes were dark with worry, grooves forming across his forehead as he looked from Lady Hayward to Selina and back again.

"You have something of importance to tell me, I understand," he said, before Selina could say a word. "Might I beg you to speak to me of it with haste, Lady Selina?" A tiny smile tugged at one corner of his mouth but faded quickly. "There are some matters that have been weighing heavily on my mind these last few hours and I must have them resolved."

Selina drew in a long breath but forced herself to speak quietly.

"Might it be to do with Lady Amelia?" she asked, as Lord Barrington frowned. "I do not mean to speak ill of your sister, Lord Barrington, nor to suggest that whatever has occurred is her fault in any way, however."

Lord Barrington snorted.

"It is *entirely* her doing," he stated, unequivocally. "It does not surprise me that you know my situation is to do solely with my sister's behavior, Lady Selina. It shames me, however."

Shaking her head, Selina tried to find a way to explain what she had overheard.

"Lord Barrington, that is not at all what I meant," she stated, trying to find a firmness that would flood into her voice. "Might I also ask if Lord Telford is involved in any way?"

This seemed to catch Lord Barrington's attention, for his eyes flared and he shifted in his chair so that he was leaning a little further forward, his gaze fixed on hers.

"You did not read my letter," Selina finished, softly. "If only you had, Lord Barrington, you might have known—"

"Your letter?" Lord Barrington barked, making her start violently. "You mean to say that you knew my sister intended to escape with this... this... rogue? You knew, somehow, that Lord Telford's friend would be the one to do this to her?"

Selina shook her head.

"No, Lord Barrington, it is not as you think!" she exclaimed, glancing towards Lady Hayward, who was watching Lord Barrington with sharp eyes, although she said nothing at all. "This was not your sister's doing. I wrote to you simply because I could not attend last evening and nor could I call, given Lady Hayward's condition. I–"

"I do not understand," Lord Barrington said, slowly, interrupting her. "You come here to tell me that my sister is *not* the one at fault, when it is she whom I discovered in the arms of a gentleman I did not know, having made her way out into the gardens rather than returning to my mother's side!" His tone had grown angry now, as though he was greatly displeased with Selina's attempts to defend his sister. "There can be nothing –"

"Lord Barrington, please!"

Before she knew what she was doing, Selina found herself on her feet, her hands flung out and the sound of her voice seeming to echo around the room. Astonishment replaced his anger on Lord Barrington's face as he looked back at her, his eyes a little wide and the paleness in his cheeks increasing just a little. Selina wanted to shrink back down into her seat, wanted to apologize for speaking so much out of turn, but a small, encouraging smile from Lady Hayward gave her the modicum of courage she required to continue.

"I overheard Lord Telford and another gentleman speaking," she said, her voice louder than she had expected. "Two nights ago. One had attempted to pull your sister far away from the rest of the guests but she had refused. This angered Lord Telford. They discussed the matter again, and I knew that they meant to try again when it came to Lady Amelia."

Lord Barrington rubbed one hand across his eyes.

"And for what purpose?"

"To gain money from you," Selina stated, firmly.

"Lord Telford stated quite clearly that this was their sole intention. I have little doubt that soon, if you have not already, you will receive a note from Lord Telford or from this other gentleman demanding a certain sum of money in order for him to remain silent and protect your sister's reputation." Slowly, she sank back down into her chair, her legs trembling slightly, but her hands clenched tight. "Your sister had nothing to do with what occurred, Lord Barrington. It was all planned by these two gentlemen in order to extract wealth from you."

For what felt like an eternity, Lord Barrington said nothing at all. He held Selina's gaze and she looked back at him without hesitation, even though her own heart was pounding with both anxiety and embarrassment at how she had spoken to him. The gentleman sighed on multiple occasions before rubbing one hand down his face, clearly a little confused.

"My sister cried into my shoulder," he said quietly, his expression now growing a little wretched. "When I found them, she was attempting to remove herself from this gentleman's grasp. I did not believe her, of course. I presumed that she was simply doing such a thing, having regretted allowing him to take her out to the garden in the first place. I never once imagined that...."

He trailed off, a groan escaping his lips as he shook his head.

"You did not believe her," Lady Hayward said gently, as Lord Barrington nodded, dropping his head. "Might I ask how she fares today?"

"She has kept to her room and will not come out," Lord Barrington replied, heavily. "I have already told the servants to begin packing her things so that she might be returned to the estate. My mother is in great distress also, believing that her daughter has made some of the most foolish choices imaginable."

"But she did not," Selina said, firmly. "I am sure that the gentleman in question forced your sister from the room, given what you say of how she responded to your presence when you found her. It was clearly relief that you had come for her, that you were present there with her. Although I expect that the damage has been done and that, very soon, you will receive a note demanding that you pay a certain sum to this gentleman in order to keep his lips sealed about what happened. No doubt he will share this with Lord Telford."

"If he does not continue to ask for more," Lady Hayward added, darkly. "There is no reason for him *not* to do so. Blackmail tends to be a never-ending thing. I am sure that most gentlemen would do anything they could to protect such a secret as this."

Selina watched as Lord Barrington let out a long breath, rose and then rang the bell.

"I did not read your letter yesterday, Lady Selina," he admitted, going to the corner of the room so that he might pour himself a drink. "I found myself quite caught up with things – ironically, things to do with my sister - and, come the evening, I thought to simply speak to you in person, so that I might apologize for being unable to read it, and to ask you what was contained within the missive."

"But you could not have known that I would be absent entirely," Selina replied softly. "That is not your fault, Lord Barrington. I quite understand."

He grimaced and made to say more, only to be interrupted when the butler tapped on the door.

"Enter."

"Should I send for tea, my Lord?"

"Yes. But also instruct the staff to stop packing away Lady Amelia's things and return everything to its place," Lord Barrington said, slowly, as the butler nodded. "And, tell me, have I received any correspondence today?"

The butler nodded.

"Indeed, my Lord."

"Bring it to me at once."

Again, the butler nodded, then stepped away, leaving Selina, Lady Hayward and Lord Barrington together once more.

"We will see if you are right, Lady Selina," Lord Barrington said, heavily. "I feel such a burden of guilt at present, for my poor sister has..."

"Now is not the time to berate yourself, Lord Barrington," Lady Hayward interrupted, gently. "Will you pay the money?"

Lord Barrington sighed and nodded.

"What else can I do?" he asked, as Selina watched the flickering emotions dart across his face. "If I do not, then I fear for what might happen to Amelia. She is my sister, as you have said, and I am entirely responsible for her. I must protect her, especially if she is not at all at fault for last evening events."

"I am sure that she is not," Selina replied, softly. "I am aware that you have found her, in the past, lacking in some respects, Lord Barrington, but last night, she was not eager to step out of doors with this gentleman. Lord

Telford told you of it in the hope that you would believe her to be entirely guilty, and would not question what you had witnessed."

This did not seem to comfort Lord Barrington.

"Then they know of my irritation and upset about my sister's conduct," he said, darkly. "And they have used it against me."

He was unable to say more, for the butler returned with a small stack of letters on a tray. Handing them to Lord Barrington, he was dismissed and closed the door tightly behind him, leaving Lord Barrington, Selina and Lady Hayward to stare down at the letters before him.

"I recognize this seal," Lord Barrington muttered, setting one note aside. "And this is an invitation, given the ribbon."

This continued on for some minutes, until he was finally left with two letters which he did not recognize.

Selina sat up straight.

"The one in your left hand is my own," she said, a flush of color hitting her cheeks. "I am sure of it."

Lord Barrington nodded, an apology in his gaze as he looked back at her.

"Then it is this one," he said, heavily, breaking open the seal of the other and unfolding it. Dropping his eyes to it, he read it swiftly before letting out a heavy sigh, telling Selina that it was, indeed the letter they had expected, the blackmail demand. "It is as you have said, Lady Selina," his words were tainted with frustration and sorrow, "Lord Havers, it seems, has demanded quite a large sum in order to keep what he has done entirely to himself."

"And if you do not pay it?" Lady Hayward asked, as Lord Barrington threw her a wretched look. "Then he will tell the *ton* everything?"

Lord Barrington raked one hand through his hair, his eyes dropping back to the letter.

"Then I believe that my sister's reputation will be quite ruined with a mixture of both truth and lies," he said, throwing the letter onto the table. "Lord Havers states that he will do whatever is required, and say whatever he needs to, in order to make certain that Amelia will never be able to lift her head in society again. She will never marry, unless it is to a gentleman in desperate need of her dowry." His eyes lifted to Selina's and she was shocked by the sheer desperation that shone there. "I have been entirely taken in," he finished, as she swallowed hard. "Just what am I to do now?"

CHAPTER EIGHT

Charles rapped quietly on the door to his sister's bedchamber.

"Amelia," he said, gently. "My dear sister, I must speak to you." There came no response and Charles closed his eyes, knowing that his sister had every right to refuse his company. "I have learned of something," he continued, speaking as firmly as he could. "Something that has proven to me that you are *not* at fault, Amelia." Leaning his head against the door, Charles let out a long breath, knowing that he had caused his sister a great deal of distress. Inadvertently, yes, but there still lingered a burden on his heart. "Please, sister," he said, a little more urgently. "Lady Selina and Lady Hayward have come to call on me. Lady Selina overheard Lord Telford and Lord Havers speaking. She knows what was done. It was planned. It was all planned. And I –" He broke off as the sound of a key scraping in the lock caused him to step back. The door opened, just a crack, and his sister peered through the gap, her eyes wide but her cheeks pale. "But I did not believe you," he finished, reaching out one hand to her. "Amelia, I am sorry."

She sniffed but did not open the door further, nor take his hand. It was clear that she had been crying for some time, for there was redness all about her eyes.

"The servants have been putting my gowns back in my wardrobe," she said, her voice hoarse. "Does that mean I am to remain in London?"

Charles kept his hand outstretched.

"It does," he told her. "Please, will you not come down with me? Lady Selina and Lady Hayward still remain and I have sent for Lord Banfield also. I think that it is important for him to be aware of this situation, for he might well be able to give us some advice." Amelia slowly began to open the door and Charles caught it, stepping aside to give her a little more space. "Mama has been asked to join us also."

"Lady – Lady Selina is here?"

The incredulity in her voice told him that she was just as astonished as he had been.

"She overheard the plan to deliberately make this situation what it was," Charles told her. "This was planned by both Lord Telford and Lord Havers, Amelia."

"For what purpose?"

Wincing, he shook his head sadly.

"To gain money from me," he said, as Amelia's hand flew to her mouth. "In order to protect your reputation, they are demanding money from me, as the price of their silence." He shrugged. "That is to say, Lord Havers is demanding it, although I am certain that Lord Telford will receive some also."

Tears began to fill Amelia's eyes and she dropped her head.

"I did try to stop him," she said, hoarsely. "I tried, Barrington, but he would not release me! And if I had screamed, then that would have drawn so much attention and I–"

"There is no need to explain, Amelia." Charles stepped forward and put one hand on his sister's arm, seeing how she flinched and cursing himself for being so unthinking. Dropping his hand, he waited until she finally lifted her head to look at him. "Please, come and join the others, Amelia. There is much to discuss and I can promise you that none present think poorly of you. Indeed, Lady Selina is most concerned for your welfare."

Amelia sniffed.

"She is kind," she said, her voice tremulous as she stepped from the room and pushed the door closed behind her. "But, Barrington, if she knew of this plan, why did she not tell you of it?" She stopped dead, her eyes wide as she looked up at him. "Why did she not prevent it?"

"She tried to," he answered, wanting to make certain that Amelia understood that Lady Selina was not at fault. "She wrote me an urgent letter, as she was prevented from attending the ball due to Lady Hayward's injury. I – I did not read the letter, Amelia. I was much too busy and, not realizing that she would not be present, thought to speak to her in person. I am sorry." His brow furrowed as he realized just how much he had to apologize for. "I am truly sorry, Amelia. I should have considered the urgency which the footman who delivered Lady Selina's note mentioned and set time aside to read it. Had I done so, then you might now be quite contented, rather than facing this problem."

Amelia let out a long breath but said nothing more. After a moment or two, she lifted her chin, straightened her shoulders and preceded him towards the drawing room. Charles followed after, a heavier burden settling over him than he had ever felt before.

"And so you are to pay this money to Lord Havers."

Charles nodded, just as his mother let out a small gasp of dismay.

"I have no other choice," he stated, as Lady Barrington's eyes widened. "If I do not, then Amelia will be unjustly punished by the *ton* for something I know that she did not do." He glanced at his sister, who was sitting by their mother, sniffing just a little as he spoke. "I cannot let such a thing occur."

Lady Selina, who had been both apologetic to Lady Amelia for not making certain that her brother had read her letter, as well as angry that she had been unable to prevent what had occurred, let out a small sigh.

"I cannot imagine that Lord Telford has chosen to do this to you only, Lord Barrington," she said, slowly. "I must confess, I think that the success of this particular endeavour will only inspire him to do more."

"It is only the first month of the Season," Lady Hayward remarked. "Therefore, he has many weeks left for him to attempt to do so again, to some other unfortunate young woman. It is not something he can simply do without due consideration and effort."

Charles frowned.

"What do you mean?"

"Lord Telford or Lord Havers must ingratiate themselves with the lady in question, as well as her companion, chaperone or parent," Lady Hayward explained. "They cannot simply meet a young lady and then steal her away in an instant! They must choose the young lady carefully, must make themselves as trustworthy and as gentlemanly as they can before attempting to convince her – as they did with Lady Amelia – to join one of them in a less than proper situation. It speaks well of you, Lady Amelia, that you did not do as Lord Havers asked."

Lady Amelia sniffed and nodded but did not smile. Charles' heart ached. He could not imagine all that his sister was feeling and to know that he had only increased her suffering made him all the more frustrated.

"If they do not succeed, then I suppose they would do as they did with Lady Amelia," Lady Selina added, quietly. "They would gain wealth either way, although the latter approach is, most likely, less than agreeable to them."

"I would agree," Lord Banfield said, firmly. "There must be a way to put an end to this, without compromising Lady Amelia's reputation."

"I do not see how," Charles' mother replied, shaking her head. "They are behaving in such a secretive manner that I am quite at a loss as to how such a thing could be prevented!"

Charles lowered his head and pinched the bridge of

his nose, trying to rid himself of the tension which flooded him. He wanted to think clearly, wanted to find an answer to the question of how to stop Lord Telford and Lord Havers' scheme, but nothing came to mind.

"For the moment, at least, you must continue on as you are, Lady Amelia." Charles looked up, seeing Lady Selina speaking gently but directly to his sister. "You must continue to go out into society, you must make it plain that you have nothing to fear or to hide. Let Lord Telford and Lord Havers see you. They might come to believe that your brother has told you nothing about the money they have requested and, therefore, you will be able to go about society just as before."

Amelia shook her head.

"I have no wish to," she replied, haltingly. "It is already too humiliating."

"You must," Charles replied, although he spoke gently. "The *ton* will notice, should you remove yourself from their company. We cannot allow whispers to be spread, Amelia. Havers' note asks that the money be paid within the sennight, so we have at least a few days before they will act in any way."

Looking earnestly at his sister, he waited until, finally, she gave a small nod, although she did not hold his gaze for long.

"We will be with you," Lord Banfield added, in an encouraging manner. "You are not alone in this predicament, Lady Amelia."

"Indeed, you are not," Lady Hayward stated, firmly. "Lady Selina and I shall be with you, as will your mother, your brother and Lord Banfield. We will support you, Lady Amelia. Of that, we give you our word."

Charles had to confess himself astonished at just how readily Lady Selina agreed to such a thing, thinking to himself that the young lady showed a remarkable character – one that he was coming to admire more with almost every day that passed. She appeared to be kind, caring and generous in spirit. The fact that she had shown so much concern for his sister, when Amelia had been both disingenuous and rude, spoke very highly of her and Charles could not help but think well of her. In fact, he conceded to himself, he did not think he knew any other young lady like her.

"We will think of something," Lady Selina finished, smiling warmly at Lady Amelia. "This has been something of a shock for many of us, remember. It is only because our shock and surprise are so very great that we now struggle to think of a way forward. I am certain it will become clear to us very soon."

"Thank you, Lady Selina," came Lady Amelia's reply. "I will do as you ask." She swallowed hard. "Are you to attend Lord Irving's soiree and card party this evening?"

Lady Selina glanced to Lady Hayward, who immediately nodded.

"Yes, of course," she answered, with Charles quickly recalling that Lady Hayward's ankle still pained her. "Lady Selina and I fully intend to be present."

The look of relief that filled Amelia's face told Charles that she needed Lady Selina to be present before she could even feel remotely comfortable with being back in the company of the *beau monde*.

"You must also prepare yourself for the fact that Lord Telford and Lord Havers might also be present, however," Lady Selina added, speaking with great gentleness. "Of course, you will have your friends with you and that will encourage you, but be aware of their presence and do not allow it to overwhelm you."

For a moment, Charles feared that his sister might collapse against their mother and refuse to attend this evening's soiree, such was her fear, but after a moment or two, Lady Amelia dragged in a shaking breath and nodded, a slight gleam of determination coming into her eyes.

"We should take our leave," Lady Hayward said, removing herself carefully from the chair and standing tall, despite the injury to her ankle. "Thank you, Lord Barrington, for allowing us to speak to you – and to the rest of you also."

"I will send out a dinner invitation so that we might converse about this matter again very soon," Charles replied, rising from his chair so that he could offer Lady Hayward his arm, given the pain to her ankle. "I do hope that you will accept?"

"Of course."

She took his arm gratefully and, after bidding the rest of them farewell, walked with him to the door. Lady Selina joined them, walking just a little behind them both, although Charles remained acutely aware of her presence.

"Thank you, Lord Barrington."

Lady Hayward took the arm of a footman and was helped carefully into the carriage, leaving Charles to turn to speak to Lady Selina. She was standing quietly just behind him, clearly waiting until her chaperone was seated before she herself climbed inside.

"Lady Selina, you cannot know of the depths of my gratitude," he told her, speaking the truth from his heart. "or of my guilt and sorrow that I did not treat your letter with the seriousness that it deserved." She did not smile at him, nor tell him that he did not need to feel any such thing. Instead, she held his gaze, as though considering what it was that she was going to say. "You are very good to my sister," he continued, as Lady Selina finally dropped her gaze. "I know that she has not always behaved correctly towards you and even I myself must have appeared rude on occasion, but –"

"That does not matter," Lady Selina interrupted, with such fervor in her voice that he looked at her in surprise. "It was an unfortunate set of circumstances which prevented me from calling upon you in person, Lord Barrington. If I had been there last evening, then I –" She broke off, shaking her head. "It does not matter. Regardless of what has occurred in the past, Lord Barrington, I am entirely committed to helping your sister in this difficult time. I cannot imagine the suffering that she must be enduring at present."

Again, there speaks her kind heart, Charles thought to himself, finding himself smiling at the lady who, after a moment, gave him a smile of her own, although a hint of color infused her cheeks as she did so. Without intending to, Charles discovered that he now held one hand out to the lady and, when she gave it to him, he bowed low over it, hoping that it spoke of his consideration and admiration for her.

"I am more grateful to you than you can know, Lady Selina," he informed her, seeing the way that her cheeks flared with color as he held her hand in his, ignoring those about them, those who might be watching what he was doing. "My sister also. And my mother."

She pressed her lips together and then returned his gaze, her hazel eyes glinting with specks of gold. A curl of her fair hair escaped from her bonnet and brushed at her temples, and with the color in her cheeks fading to a delicate pink, Charles found himself suddenly overwhelmed with the beauty of the lady.

"You are all more than welcome, Lord Barrington," she said, graciously. "Although I fear that I do not deserve such gratitude. It was only fate which permitted me to overhear the truth of Lord Havers and Lord Telford's plans."

"But you did not have to share it," he answered her. "You did not have to speak of it to me. You might have chosen to allow things to progress as they were meant to and, instead, focused on seeking out your own happiness."

She frowned.

"I hope that I should never have such a selfish heart," she responded, making Charles smile.

"Your heart is to be greatly admired, given its kindness, consideration and sweetness," he found himself saying, seeing how Lady Selina's blush increased again as she looked away. "You will find my gratitude and my thankfulness only increasing, Lady Selina. I pray that we will be able to find a solution to this dreadful circumstance."

"As do I, Lord Barrington," Lady Selina replied, sincerity ringing through her voice. "As do I."

MAKING his way into the drawing room, Charles bowed to greet their host for the evening, feeling his sister tense as her hand rested on his arm. She curtsied quickly and then rose once more, with both Lord and Lady Irving greeting her warmly. There was no hint of mockery in their voice or their words which, he hoped, would be an encouragement to Amelia. She had been afraid that, somehow, the knowledge of what had occurred between Lord Havers and herself would be well known, even though Charles had promised her that he had already replied to Lord Havers and promised to pay what had been asked for.

"Please, enjoy this evening!" Lady Irving exclaimed. "The card games are in the next room, but you are also welcome to linger here."

"Thank you," Charles replied, making his way into the room a little more and looking around him.

He, as well as his sister, had to make it plain to the entirety of the *ton* that there was nothing to concern him this evening, that he had no anxiety or concern over this particular situation – that, in fact, there was no situation at all. The truth was, of course, that he was greatly anxious over his sister and worried about her reaction should she see Lord Telford or Lord Havers, but he had to hide all of that from his expression and manner.

"There, you see?" he heard his mother say, as she walked beside Amelia. "They have nothing to say about you. Everything is just as it was."

"Indeed it is," Charles agreed, smiling warmly at Amelia, even though he knew his own heart was swirling with tension. "Look, there is Lady Selina with Lady Hayward, talking to Lord Banfield. She has seen you, Amelia. Go and join her."

His mother shot him a quick look.

"Will you join us?"

Charles shook his head.

"In a few minutes," he said, quietly. "I want to see who else might be present this evening."

Seeing the knowing look on his mother's face, Charles gave her a quick smile and then stepped away, relieved that his sister would be in good company. Clearing his throat and collecting a drink from a passing footman, he made his way slowly through the room and then through the door into the room where the card games were to be held.

The instant he stepped inside, his heart slammed hard against his chest. There stood not only Lord Havers but Lord Telford, talking quietly together in the corner of the room. His brow lowered, his anger began to burn and, without thinking, he turned sharply on his heel and made his way around the edge of the room towards them.

Lord Telford, who had been looking rather thoughtful, caught sight of him and rearranged his features from an expression of dark consideration to geniality.

"Good evening, Lord Barrington," he said, in a cheerful tone of voice which clashed hard against Charles' anger. "And how do you fare this evening?"

"Spare me your false pretenses," Charles growled, wishing that he could plant them both a facer. "I am well aware, Telford, that you are as much in this scheme as Lord Havers."

Nothing was said in response to this for a moment, although Lord Telford's expression of surprise lingered for a short time.

"Pretense?" he said, as Charles' anger grew into a roaring fire. "I know nothing of what you speak."

"You know very well!" Charles exclaimed, before forcing himself to keep his voice low. He could not risk being overheard. "You are together in this situation, are you not? You both seek to take money from me by blackmail. There is no need to feign your innocence, Lord Telford. I am fully aware of your involvement."

Lord Telford's expression remained innocently surprised for a moment or two longer but, after looking into Charles' face for another short while, he eventually sighed and shook his head.

"Very well, then," he said, with a shrug. "You are aware of us both."

Lord Havers chuckled, his tone dark.

"But you have already agreed to give us what we ask, Lord Barrington, and I confess that I am greatly looking forward to receiving it!"

"So that you might share it between yourself and Lord Telford," Charles bit out, barely able to hold onto his temper. "Before you then consider which other unfortunate young lady to chase after!"

"Or we may keep requesting money from you!" Lord Havers responded, gleefully. "Have you never thought of that, Lord Barrington?"

The laugh that came from him was cold and sent a chill straight through Charles' heart, cooling his anger somewhat. Lady Hayward had, it seemed, been right in her suspicions of their intent.

Lord Telford tilted his head.

"And I must wonder how you came to know of my involvement, Lord Barrington," he said, slowly, as Charles gritted his teeth to keep from biting out a harsh retort. "How you were so certain of it that you had no doubts whatsoever when you spoke to me."

A vision of Lady Selina filled Charles' head, making dread fill his heart.

"I was not fooled by you," he stated, angrily. "That was all, Telford. You might believe that your behavior was that of a supposedly innocent man, but do not think that I missed the gleam in your eye or the falseness of your smile."

This did not appear to convince Lord Telford, however, for the calculating, considering look in his eye did not fade. Instead, he merely held Charles' gaze, his lips a little thin and his eyes narrowed.

"I will pay you this time, Lord Havers, but I shall not do so again," Charles finished, trying to distract Lord Telford from what he had said. "I shall not be blackmailed!"

"We will see," Lord Havers replied, with a dark smile.

"I have come to learn that a gentleman will do anything for those he claims to care about. And I suspect, Lord Barrington, that you will do a great deal to protect your sister."

"And any others you have come to care about," Lord Telford added, making Charles' frown deepen all the more. "I think we have said enough for this evening, Lord Barrington." He cleared his throat and inclined his head mockingly, a grin plastered across his face. "Good evening."

Charles watched them go, unable to give any retort, as a feeling of dread continued to make its way through him. He had, it seemed unwittingly, managed to invoke Lord Telford's suspicions and, given Lady Selina's new closeness to Lady Amelia as well as to himself, Charles feared that it would not be long before Lord Telford might come to realize that she had been the one to inform him of Telford's involvement.

He dropped his head and let out a long, heavy breath. Just what had he done?

CHAPTER NINE

"Do you think they are here this evening?"

Selina smiled and squeezed Lady Amelia's arm gently.

"I am sure they are," she said, gently, "but there is nothing to fear."

Lady Amelia let out a long breath and nodded, although Selina could practically feel the tension pouring out of her. It had been a little over a sennight since Selina had appeared at Lord Barrington's home and demanded to speak to him, and since that time, Lady Amelia had been by her side at almost every social occasion. Selina had no concerns about their increasing friendship, however and was, in fact, a little grateful for it. Whilst Lady Amelia was certainly not anything like her own sister, Anna, it was encouraging for Selina to have a friend standing close by her at social occasions. Lady Amelia's character had changed significantly, although Selina was sorry to see her anxiety and her worry. Whilst it was important for Lady Amelia to behave with all propriety – something she was doing now without hesitation or argument – Selina did hope that some of the confidence and happiness she had seen in Lady Amelia before would return.

"My brother states that he has heard from Lord Havers," Lady Amelia said, quietly. "He told me so this morning."

Selina swallowed hard, feeling her anxiety begin to rise up within her.

"Indeed?"

"The money has been received but he has been warned that more might be required," Lady Amelia replied, her shoulders slumping as she looked towards Selina. "It seems I am not to be freed of this. Nor my brother."

"That is not your doing," Selina assured her. "Now, there are bound to be many excellent gentlemen seeking your company this evening. Will you dance?"

Lady Amelia drew in a long, shaky breath.

"Should I?"

"Of course!" Selina exclaimed, as Lady Barrington nodded. "Your mother will be watching you carefully so there is no need for concern."

"And mayhap I might be the first to ask for such a thing?"

Selina turned to see none other than Lord Banfield standing just to their left, a broad smile settling across his face – although it was not directed towards her. Rather, he was looking to Lady Amelia who, after a moment, let out a heavy sigh but, in doing so, also allowed herself to smile.

"As always, Lord Banfield, you are ready at the first to offer your companionship," Lady Amelia said, as Selina let go of her arm and took a small step back, sharing a glance with Lady Barrington. "I would be glad of your company, thank you."

Lord Banfield and Lady Amelia continued to speak as Selina looked away, allowing them both as much privacy as she could. Lord Banfield was being particularly attentive to Lady Amelia this last sennight and, whilst Selina knew Lady Amelia was glad of it, she could not help but wonder if the gentleman had any true feelings of affection for the lady.

"And are you dancing this evening, Lady Selina?"

"I am," Selina replied, smiling. Handing him her dance card, she thanked him and looked down to see that her cotillion was to be with Lord Banfield. She had little doubt, however, that Lady Amelia would have two dances taken by Lord Banfield and wondered if one might be the waltz. Although two dances was verging on a declaration, Banfield's close friendship with Barrington would likely change most people's view of it.

"Should you be willing to give me your dance card also, Lady Selina, I should like to peruse it."

A familiar voice floated towards her and she turned her head to see Lord Barrington coming towards them, his eyes warm as he smiled at her.

"Unless, that is, you have already had your dance card filled up entirely?"

"I have only just arrived, Lord Barrington," she replied, with a chuckle. "But yes, I would be glad to offer you my dance card."

Aware of the spreading warmth through her chest, she quickly gave her dance card to Lord Barrington and concentrated solely on keeping herself entirely composed.

Lady Hayward shot her a quick look but Selina ignored it completely. She had yet to admit to Lady Hayward that, having been often in Lord Barrington's company this last week, much to her own astonishment, she had found herself eagerly looking forward to being so again. Yes, the circumstances that they faced were very dreadful indeed, and she did not wish to make light of them in any way, but Lord Barrington was a kind-hearted, handsome and respectful gentleman and she enjoyed his company immensely. And to dance with him brought with it a fresh wave of delight.

"The waltz?" he murmured, as though he wished for only her to hear. Her heart pounded at the thought of being held in his arms. "I do hope that is satisfactory, Lady Selina."

"Of course," she said, softly, accepting it back from him. Looking into his face, she saw the flicker of concern which still lingered in his eyes – a concern that had not left him since she had told him the truth about his sister. "Might I ask, Lord Barrington, whether or not Lord Havers or Lord Telford are present this evening?"

"They are," he replied, darkly. "Do be on your guard, Lady Selina."

She frowned at this.

"Your sister should be so, Lord Barrington, but as for myself, I do not see –"

He swiped the air in front of her with his hand.

"They are searching for the next young lady they might accost," he said, warning her. "What is to say it is not you?"

Selina shook her head.

"I am sure that I would not be chosen, given my friendship with Lady Amelia," she said, firmly. "Lord Telford would not consider it, given that surely, as he would expect, you would have spoken to me of his deceit and manipulation."

Lord Barrington looked away before clearing his throat hard, shaking his head as he did so.

"I believe, Lady Selina, that he is a man capable of a great many things," he replied, slowly. "You must be careful."

Selina frowned, holding Lord Barrington's gaze and wondering if there was more to his words than he was able to express at present. However, he said nothing more and she was only able to nod and thank him for his concern, although her worries and her questions still remained within her heart.

"LADY SELINA, GOOD EVENING."

Selina's stomach dropped to the floor but she forced herself into a curtsey as none other than Lord Telford bowed first to Lady Hayward and then to her.

"Good evening, Lord Telford," she replied, doing all she could to keep her expression one of amiability. "I do hope that you are enjoying this evening?"

He smiled at her, tilting his head just a little.

"I would enjoy it all the more if you would be willing to allow me a dance, Lady Selina," he said, gesturing to her dance card. "Or am I much too late?"

Selina hesitated, looking down at her dance card and wishing that she had the confidence to tell Lord Telford that she had no desire to dance with him and that, therefore, she would rather he did not.

"No?" Lord Telford asked, now looking rather delighted. "Then I do hope you will allow me to take whichever dance you have remaining."

Swallowing hard, Selina forced a smile to her lips and then tugged her dance card from her wrist. She did not give it to him straight away however, aware of Lady Hayward's presence beside her and using that encouragement to find a little strength for herself. "I believe that one dance would be suitable, Lord Telford," she said, as firmly as she could, "for we would not wish to give people the wrong impression, and I am rather fatigued this evening."

It was a poor excuse and, as the smile slid from Lord Telford's face, she knew that he was aware of her true feelings. It was clear that she did not wish to be in his company for long. Hopefully, he would consider it a result of her first introduction to him, when he had made such eager advances towards Miss Newington and Lady Amelia.

"The country dance," he said crisply, looking at her directly as a thin smile pulled at his lips, a darkness in his eyes that made Selina shudder inwardly. "One I hope you will enjoy, Lady Selina."

Selina murmured something quiet and Lord Telford

stepped away, but not without shooting her a hard glance and a dark scowl. Lady Hayward watched him with an equally hard gaze before she turned to Selina.

"I do not like the idea of you dancing with Lord Telford, Lady Selina," she said, as Selina let out a long breath. "You could easily have refused him."

A little ashamed of her lack of courage, Selina nodded.

"I am aware I could have done such a thing, Lady Hayward, but I lacked the strength of will. After all, it would be perceived as remarkably rude to refuse a gentleman, when I still have dances unclaimed."

Lady Hayward nodded, a sympathetic look crossing her face.

"I shall not reprimand you, for you are right that others would see it as rude," she said, softly. "But I am inclined to agree with Lord Barrington. You must be on your guard."

Selina smiled tightly.

"I will," she promised, knowing that Lady Hayward would be watching her also. "And let us hope that the dance will be of short duration!"

"Shall we, Lady Selina?"

Taking Lord Telford's arm, Selina suppressed a shudder and stepped out with him onto the dance floor.

"I am inclined to believe that you do not wish to be here with me, Lady Selina," Lord Telford said, his voice low and grating. "Is there some particular reason?"

Recalling the shame that had come with her lack of courage already, Selina forced herself to speak with as much honesty as she dared.

"Do you not recall the first time we were introduced, Lord Telford?" she asked, lifting her chin as she spoke to him, although she kept her gaze averted. "I am surprised that you would expect me to think well of you after such behavior."

Lord Telford snorted with derision.

"I did nothing untoward, Lady Selina," he said, a sneer pulling at his mouth. "Lady Amelia chose to come into the room without her brother *or* Lady Barrington – it cannot be that you would think me responsible for that?"

"I think you responsible for even approaching Lady Amelia when she was without proper chaperonage, regardless of whether she had chosen to be in that room alone or not," Selina replied, her heart beating so loudly that she was certain Lord Telford could hear it. "I cannot think well of you, Lord Telford."

She spoke more honestly than she had ever done before to Lord Telford – and she could tell from the way his jaw set that she had angered him. Her stomach twisted, her anxiety growing steadily and, as the dance began, Selina felt herself almost overcome with nervousness. Part of her feared that Lord Telford would do something so improper, and yet so overt that everyone present would know of it, whereas another part worried that he would not return her to Lady Hayward when the dance came to an end. Would there be punishment for her words of honesty to him? Would he think of something he might do to make certain that she was humiliated in retaliation?

The dance progressed and Selina found herself remaining entirely silent as they went through the steps. Neither she nor Lord Telford shared a word with each other, and nor did he even attempt to smile at her. They must have looked as though they were the most miserable of all the dancers, although Selina was doing her best to keep her composure, to not give in to the spiraling fear within her heart.

Lady Hayward is watching me, she told herself, over and over again. *There is nothing to be worried about. I will return to her side and all will be well.*

The end of the dance came and Selina curtsied as Lord Telford bowed. He offered his arm and she accepted reluctantly, expecting to be turned towards Lady Hayward once more.

Lord Telford did not do as she had expected.

"It is a very great shame that you do not think well of me, Lady Selina," he said, beginning to walk with her in the opposite direction, pulling her away from Lady Hayward. "I assure you, I am quite amiable."

Selina's heart began to pound furiously as panic took hold. The other dancers were beginning to disperse and she felt herself trapped as Lord Telford continued to lead her away from Lady Hayward. Attempting to pull her hand from his arm, she heard his dark laugh as he placed his hand over her wrist, keeping her beside him.

"If you are attempting to make a more favorable impression, Lord Telford, then I can assure you that you are failing entirely," she replied, slowly her steps and forcing him to do so also. "Unhand me!"

Lord Telford chuckled and Selina's panic grew. She looked all about her, praying that Lady Hayward would come after her, would have seen her difficulty, for unless she screamed and fought Lord Telford – which would, of course, cause a great scene and, no doubt, have Lord Telford exclaim that he had been merely returning her to her chaperone and had no understanding of her behavior – she was trapped beside him.

"It was you, I suppose," Lord Telford continued, his voice now low and filled with malice. "It was *you* who informed Lord Barrington about my involvement in the matter with his sister?" He looked at her and smiled grimly. "Yes, I have noticed your closeness with Lady Amelia these last few days. How extraordinary, given that there was no such friendship between you before? I –"

"That is enough, Lord Telford!"

Selina came to a halt, using every bit of strength she had to remain steadfast as he attempted to tug her forward. She stumbled but continued to do her utmost to remain where she was, with Lord Telford's face darkening with every moment that passed. They were now very close to the other guests, the dance floor cleared entirely, and others now moving towards it, to form up for the next dance set, but Selina knew that she could not permit herself to be taken any further. Quite what Lord Telford now intended, she did not know, but it was not as though she wished to find out! If her resisting him was noticed, people would talk, but she feared that less than what would happen if she allowed him his way.

"Unhand me," she bit out, her breathing coming more quickly as she fought to remain steady, with Lord Telford glaring down at her as he tried to have her walk forward. "I will not –"

"I should do as the lady asks."

Selina felt her whole body sag with relief as the voice of Lord Barrington reached her ears. Lord Telford stopped attempting to force her to walk forward, but turned sharply, which movement made Selina stumble forward a few steps.

A strong hand caught her arm and she looked up into Lord Barrington's face. It was dark with anger.

"Release her, Telford," he said and, much to Selina's relief, the gentleman did so – although she was certain that, had he any other choice, he would have refused entirely.

"I was merely searching for Lady Hayward!" Lord Telford exclaimed, his wide eyes and spread hands speaking of nothing more than innocence. "I cannot understand you, Lord Barrington!"

"Lady Hayward has been held back from coming after her charge by one Lord Havers," Lord Barrington replied, as Selina gasped with horror. "He was quite determined to keep her where she was, refusing to move from her side and indeed, stepping in front of her when she attempted to depart from him. How glad I am that I saw her distress and realized what was occurring."

Lord Telford's eyes narrowed, his jaw tightened and his shoulders lifted just a fraction.

"I think we will be writing to you again, come the morrow, Lord Barrington," he said, his words threatening and cruel. "There was no need for you to become involved with this matter, but now, it seems, you are eager to protect both your sister *and* Lady Selina! That, of course, must incur another payment."

Selina gasped and made to protest, but Lord Barrington reached out and took her hand, pressing it tightly with his own so that she lapsed into silence.

"You will not succeed, Telford," he stated.

Selina closed her eyes and drew in a long breath so that she might steady herself and regain her composure. It would not do to have the *ton* notice her in her present state.

"I do not see how you can prevent my success," Lord Telford replied, with a shrug. "Good evening, Lord Barrington." He swept into an ostentatious bow. "And to you, Lady Selina. I do hope our conversation will not be so interrupted again."

Selina shuddered as he walked away, her eyes lingering on the gentleman as though she wanted to make quite certain that he had left her side.

"I am sorry that I did not notice your predicament sooner, Lady Selina," Lord Barrington said, turning to her, his blue eyes swirling like the dark clouds of a storm. "I do hope that you are unharmed?"

"I am quite all right," she assured him, seeing the concern in his face and wanting immediately to reassure him. "But Lady Hayward?"

"Is waiting for you," he said, offering her his arm. "I must apologize, Lady Selina, for allowing Lord Telford to notice your nearness to Lady Amelia. I am sure that—"

"It was not your fault," she interrupted, as they began to walk around the room towards Lady Hayward once more. "Surely you cannot place any sort of blame on yourself for that!"

Lord Barrington fell silent for a few moments and Selina's heart tightened as she saw him frown. Just what had he said?

"I told Lord Telford that I knew he was involved with Lord Havers," the gentleman replied, after a very long few minutes. "I was very emphatic about my knowledge of it, rather than expressing a belief or a supposition. Therefore, Lord Telford assumed that someone knew of his connection to Lord Havers and had informed me of it." His eyes drifted to hers for a moment before snapping away again. "I believe that it did not take him long to realize that it was, most likely, you who had done so. If I had not been so foolish in my speech, then he might never have made that assumption."

Selina frowned hard, her hand still on Lord Barrington's arm. She could practically feel the strain within him, as though it was effusing from his very bones. She could understand his regret, certainly, but she herself held no such ill will.

"I am sure that Lord Telford might have come to such a conclusion himself, in time," she answered, seeing Lady Hayward's white face only a short distance away. She smiled warmly so as to reassure her chaperone, who then closed her eyes in great relief. "Lord Telford stated that he had noticed how close a friendship Lady Amelia and I had developed of late." Slowing her steps, she looked up at Lord Barrington again. "You must not allow yourself to think so poorly of your behavior, Lord Barrington. I do not have any ill will toward you."

Lord Barrington let out a long breath, nodded and thanked her.

"You have such a great kindness within you, Lady Selina," he said, quietly. "My sister has come to consider you a great friend and I–"

He broke off suddenly and Selina looked up at him, their steps slowing all the more.

"And you, Lord Barrington?"

"I..."

"Selina!"

There was no time for him to finish what he had been about to say and, whilst Selina was greatly relieved to be back by Lady Hayward's side, there came a swell of disappointment that crushed her heart. Lord Barrington cleared his throat and allowed himself a small smile as Lady Hayward thanked him profusely for what he had done, before making certain that Selina was not harmed in any way.

"I am quite well, Lady Hayward," Selina assured her, as her chaperone closed her eyes again in apparent relief. "Lord Barrington came to my side at the very moment that I most needed help."

"You were doing all you could to stop Lord Telford yourself, Lady Selina," Lord Barrington replied, sending a smile to Selina's face as she glanced up at him. "You were courageous indeed."

His words made Selina's smile grow all the more, as

Lady Hayward reached out to press her hand, clearly overwrought now with both relief and the aftermath of fear.

"I am so very glad that you are returned without harm," the lady murmured, as Selina smiled back at Lord Barrington. "Thank you, Lord Barrington."

"Yes," Selina added. "Thank you for watching for me, for coming to my aid. I do not think that I could have escaped Lord Telford without you."

Lord Barrington inclined his head, although when he lifted it again, his eyes remained fixed on hers, something now held within his gaze that Selina could not quite make out.

"And I shall continue to do so," he promised, his words swelling Selina's heart in a manner that she had not expected. "I shall do so until this threat is gone, Lady Selina. Of that, you have my word."

CHAPTER TEN

"If you frown any harder, I believe you will terrify anyone who approaches!"

Charles looked up sharply from where he had been staring, realizing that he had been doing nothing more than staring into the fire rather than being aware of anyone else around him.

"Banfield," he muttered, gesturing to an empty chair. "Join me, if you wish."

"Join you in your brooding?" Banfield replied, with a small smile. "Very well, but I confess I shall not be permitting such dark thoughts as you have at present to linger in *my* mind."

Charles allowed himself a small smile and quickly caught the attention of a footman, ordering two glasses of their best brandy. White's was quite busy this evening and Charles was grateful for it, feeling as though any conversation he was expected to have would have done nothing to lift his spirits.

"Might I ask if it is Lady Selina that occupies your thoughts?"

Snapping his head to the right, Charles fixed his gaze on Lord Banfield who, rather than apologize or look in any way contrite, arched one eyebrow and waited for Charles to reply.

He did not quite know what to say. The truth was that, yes, he had been thinking solely of Lady Selina, for the look on her face when he had found her last evening with Lord Telford had been one that he could not now remove from his thoughts. Even though tonight's social occasion had gone very well indeed – for it had been a small gathering of friends and acquaintances at Lord and Lady Borthwick's townhouse, and Lord Telford and Lord Havers had *not* been on the guest list – he had found himself continuing to consider Lady Selina.

"You do not answer me."

"I have no need to," Charles replied, speaking a little more sharply than he had intended. "Surely you must know that I have a good many concerns on my mind at present!"

Banfield chuckled.

"And one of those concerns is Lady Selina," he said, as though he knew that Charles was steadfastly refusing to state such a thing. "I do not blame you, Barrington. She is a very lovely creature and, being the daughter of a Duke, she is more than suitable as a match for you."

The protest that jumped to Charles' lips the moment Banfield finished speaking was only held back with great effort. Everything in him wanted to deny that he had any sort of consideration for Lady Selina but to do so would go against the steadily increasing regard he had for her within his heart.

"There is no shame in admitting such a thing," Banfield continued, a little more quietly. "She is quite an extraordinary young lady, and I doubt very much that you should find another like her in all of London!"

Charles' brows lowered as he studied his friend.

"It sounds as though you are a little taken with her yourself, Banfield," he replied, his heart quickening just a little as he spoke. "If you are considering her, then I shall not –"

Banfield laughed, cutting Charles off quickly.

"My dear Barrington, I have no consideration for Lady Selina in *that* particular regard," he said, sending such a crashing wave of relief over Charles that he was forced to take in a deep breath, surprising even himself by just how much he felt. "In fact, I believe I have found a young lady that I am considering."

Charles' interest was piqued immediately.

"Oh?" he repeated, looking back at Banfield, his brow lifting. "And who might that be?"

Banfield's response was held back for a moment by the return of the footman. With glass in hand, Charles gestured for his friend to continue, truly eager to know who the gentleman had discovered. These last two weeks, Banfield had done nothing other than be near Lady Amelia, and whilst Charles had been very grateful for his increased attention towards his sister, he had been anxious that his friend was missing his own opportunities to meet other young ladies, given that he wanted very much to wed.

"If you do not take kindly to my interest in this particular young lady, I shall quite understand," Banfield replied, slowly, although his brow furrowed and he looked away from Charles. "Indeed, I would be quite understanding, regardless of how I might feel myself."

Charles frowned.

"I do not understand, Banfield. I—"

"It is Lady Amelia."

Banfield's words seemed to hang in the air between them, until Charles could hardly breathe. His eyes widened and he looked back at Banfield with shock rushing through him, whilst his friend merely shrugged and then, after a few moments, looked away.

Charles could not quite take in what his friend had said. Banfield was taken with Charles' sister? Yes, he had known Lady Amelia for longer than any other gentleman of the *ton,* but surely that meant that he knew all of her foibles, her faults and failings? Never once had he expected a gentleman such as Banfield to consider the flighty, foolish lady that was his sister.

"I do not understand," Charles replied, after taking a sip of his brandy. "Amelia? You are considering her?"

"We – we are considering each other," Banfield replied, slowly. "There has been an acquaintance between us for some time, as you know, but in the last two weeks our friendship has grown steadily. I have found myself eager for her company, and she the same for mine."

"But it is Amelia!" Charles protested, weakly. "I have spoken to you of her many times, have told you all of the frustrations and difficulties that I have had to endure because of her! Surely, Banfield, you can see the truth of her character?"

Banfield said nothing for a few moments, although the look in his eyes told Charles that he had, in some way, upset his friend. A swirl of confusion broke through his mind and he let out a long breath, rubbing one hand over his forehead.

"Do you not believe, Barrington, that your sister can change her ways?" Banfield asked softly, as Charles frowned hard. "The incident with Lord Telford has struck a warning note within her, and made her consider her behavior and her manner. She has spoken to me of her sorrow at causing you so much pain and frustration and, quite frankly, Barrington, I believe her to be truthful." He shrugged. "If you do not, then I can understand your reasons for it but I will state, quite plainly, that you are wrong."

Charles' frown began to lift as a slight stab of guilt jabbed at his heart.

"I – I had not considered that," he said, honestly. "But can you be speaking the truth, Banfield?" He searched his friend's face and saw nothing but honesty there. "You have come to care for Amelia?"

"I should like to court her," Banfield replied, honestly. "I have asked her for her opinion also, of course, and she has begged me to seek your approval first." A smile tugged at the corner of his mouth. "I believe that she is greatly concerned about what you will think of her."

Blowing out a long breath, and letting the surprise of what his friend had asked sink into his heart, Charles raked one hand through his hair again and then, after a moment, nodded.

"Very well!" he exclaimed, as Banfield grinned. "I am sorry, Banfield, that I did not appear delighted immediately. I confess that I am still a little overcome with surprise at your request, but I shall not hold you back from my sister, if that is truly something you both wish for."

"It is," Banfield replied, with such a broad smile that Charles could not help but grin. "And should it all work out as I hope, then Lady Amelia will be free of Lord Telford and Lord Havers' manipulations within a few short months."

Charles took a moment to realize what his friend meant.

"You mean to marry her," he said, slowly, his grin fading just a little. "And that way, she will be free from Lord Telford's manipulations."

"That is my intention with courtship, yes," Banfield replied, with a chuckle. "And whilst it does not prevent Lord Telford from doing the same to others, it does mean that he cannot hold Lady Amelia, or you, tight in his hand any longer."

"No," Charles agreed, slowly, looking away from his friend and returning his gaze to the fire which still burned merrily in the grate. "It does not. And that is a very great relief, Banfield, for I still have no solution as to what we might do to prevent Lord Telford and Lord Havers from doing as they wish."

Banfield's smile began to fade as he lifted his brandy glass to his mouth.

"Nor I, I confess," he replied, with a shake of his head. "They appear to have the upper hand."

Charles let out another great sigh and shook his head, wishing that he had come to some sort of conclusion about the matter.

"I have put Lady Selina in danger also," he muttered, a little ashamed. "After last evening, I now expect to receive a note requesting further funds in order for them to remain silent about my sister – and all because I prevented Lord Telford from taking Lady Selina far from her chaperone."

Seeing Banfield's confusion and recalling that he had not yet told his friend about what had happened, Charles quickly told the tale. He did not fail to mention that he had lost his temper and had practically thrown accusations at Lord Telford, such that there had been very little doubt in the gentleman's mind that someone must have known of his and Lord Havers discussions.

"You cannot blame yourself," Banfield said, once Charles had finished. "I am certain that Lady Selina does not."

"No, she does not," Charles replied, with a wry smile. "She should be holding me responsible, of course, but she does not do so. Instead, she is kind and generous of spirit, which is just as I would expect from the lady." Banfield's brow rose but he said nothing. "If there was a way for me to return the very same to Lord Telford as he gives to others, then I would do so in an instant," Charles finished, heavily. "But as it stands, my mind simply cannot come up with any solution."

Banfield took another sip of his brandy and then

turned quickly back towards Charles. His eyes widened and leaning forward, he reached across to slap his hand down on the arm of Charles' chair.

"That is it precisely, old boy!"

Charles frowned.

"What do you mean?"

"To do the very same to him, as Lord Telford does to others!" Banfield exclaimed, excitement filling him. "The gentleman must be lured into a trap, the like of that which he has designed for others to fall into. Lord Havers also! We must find a situation where they are caught in a compromising circumstance, one way or the other and, in doing so, we will have enough hold over them to make certain that they do not do any such thing again!" Charles let the idea rush through his mind for a moment or two before, slowly, he began to nod. "I do not know what such a situation could be," Banfield continued, speaking very quickly indeed, as though he had to have his thoughts spoken before they flew from him. "But I am certain that, together, we might think of something!"

"And there would be a good deal still to plan, given that we would have to somehow convince both gentlemen to place themselves in such a situation without any awareness that they might be in danger," Charles added, as Banfield nodded fervently. "But you are correct to state that they would not be able to return to what they have been doing thus far, if we were to seize control of such a situation." The idea began to blossom in his mind, sending a surge of hope all through Charles. "I am aware, of course, that you would be protecting Amelia should she become your wife, but I do not want

Lord Telford and Havers to continue on this path, regardless of just how protected my own sister might be."

"Neither do I," Banfield replied, firmly. "Might I suggest, then, that we discuss the matter over dinner tomorrow evening? Lady Hayward and Lady Selina are still attending, are they not?"

Charles nodded, his sense of brooding melancholy leaving him at once.

"They are," he said, as Banfield nodded in satisfaction. "Finally, it feels as though we are in control."

"All we need now is a real plan," Banfield quipped, as Charles chuckled. "But I am sure that, come the morrow, we will have something in place."

"I have little doubt of it," Charles replied, grinning. "Lord Telford will find himself entirely undone – and I, for one, shall be very glad to see it."

"Lady Selina."

The way she smiled up at him made Charles' stomach twist as a flush of heat began to rise up his neck. There was such a beauty about her that he could hardly take it in, knowing that her character was one of kindness, of consideration and of generosity. The flecks of gold he had seen before in her hazel eyes were all the more obvious this evening, reflecting the light from the candles and making his breath catch in his chest.

"Good evening, Lord Barrington," she replied, as Lady Hayward moved to speak to his mother, leaving them to converse alone. "Thank you for inviting us this evening."

He inclined his head in the desperate hope of hiding the heat which had climbed into his cheeks.

"But of course," he replied, looking back at her. "I am very glad you are able to join us. I have come to greatly appreciate your company."

Her cheeks colored just a little and she dropped her gaze for a moment.

"You have not seen Lord Telford again, I hope?" he asked, as Lady Selina shook her head. "I hope that, this evening, we will be able to discuss a way forward with this matter. A way that will make certain that Lord Telford cannot continue with such dark intentions."

Lady Selina blinked, then smiled.

"Oh, I should be very glad to hear of any suggestions!" she exclaimed, as Charles smiled at her obvious eagerness. "I do hope I will be able to contribute something, of course. Lady Amelia has become something of a friend and I confess that I am very concerned for her." Her eyes drifted towards where Lady Amelia and Lord Banfield stood, talking quietly together. "Although," Lady Selina continued slowly, allowing her gaze to rest upon Charles once more. "I have wondered if she has more of a protector in Lord Banfield?"

Charles looked towards his sister and saw Banfield press Lady Amelia's hand for just a moment, before releasing it. There was a happiness in his heart that had not been there before, a happiness that he was now glad to share.

"It seems that Banfield has taken something of a

liking to my sister, even though he has known her for some time," he said, as Lady Selina's eyes flared. "He asked me only last evening if he might be permitted to court her."

Lady Selina pressed one hand to her heart.

"And what did you answer him, Lord Barrington?" Her eyes widened and she dropped her head. "Forgive me, that was not a question I should have asked. It is an entirely private matter, of course."

Charles laughed softly and Lady Selina looked up.

"My dear Lady Selina, you have nothing to apologize for," he said, warmly. "And you have every right to ask, given that you have become so closely acquainted with my sister – something I am very grateful for."

Lady Selina said nothing, but lifted her eyes to his, clearly waiting in anticipation for what he would say about Lord Banfield.

"And, of course," he continued, "I told Banfield that I should be very happy indeed for him to court my sister. I believe that he is an excellent gentleman and, whilst I will confess myself surprised that such an intimacy has grown between them, I am very glad indeed for the connection."

"As am I," Lady Selina replied, surprising Charles somewhat. Evidently, it seemed, his sister had spoken to Lady Selina of her eagerness for Banfield's courtship before it had even been mentioned to him! "I believe they will do very well together," she finished, as Charles nodded.

"I could not agree more," he said, just as dinner was announced.

Offering her his arm, he waited as she looked up in surprise, before accepting with a glad smile. Together, they walked through to the dining room to sit down for dinner.

～

"AND SO, we must find a way to ensure that Lord Telford and Lord Havers are *themselves* found in a situation where they cannot escape without great consequence," Lord Banfield finished as the others listened. "We have not yet been able to think of such a situation, however."

Charles nodded as the others glanced at each other, clearly thinking hard.

"Might they be tempted with a gamble?" Lady Hayward suggested, as Charles' mother nodded fervently. "I know that many gentlemen might be willing to do such a thing."

"I do not think they would do so," Lady Selina replied, her cheeks coloring as everyone looked at her at once. "They are very eager to keep the wealth that they have gained for themselves, before going out to seek more. Surely they would not, therefore, be willing to gamble some of it away?"

"I am inclined to agree with you there," Charles rumbled as Banfield rubbed his chin thoughtfully. "And such a situation might appear much too obvious."

"They will be on their guard," Lady Barrington said slowly. "They will be aware, Barrington, that you are most displeased and might wish to retaliate in some fashion."

"Which means it cannot appear to come from you," Lady Selina added, as Lady Barrington nodded. "They must believe that they have the upper hand. That they are in control."

Charles hesitated, an idea beginning to form in the very edges of his mind.

"Might I suggest, then," he said, speaking quietly, "that we place a bet in White's betting book?"

He looked to Banfield, who frowned.

"Is betting not the same as gambling?" Lady Amelia asked, but Charles shook his head.

"A bet can be made on any given subject, - it is not always a matter in which chance plays a part, but may be something where skill or other influences may affect the outcome," he said, slowly. "And if you are quite determined that you can achieve whatever the bet requires, then a vast deal of money is within your grasp. And given that both gentlemen are eager to add to their wealth, it would seem that their willingness to achieve such a thing might overtake their sensible considerations."

Everyone nodded, but there still remained a great many questions which Charles knew he would have to answer.

"What bet is it that you are thinking of presenting to them?" Banfield asked, as a murmur or interest ran around the table. "It will have to be something they can achieve."

Charles' heart began to burn in his chest as he glanced towards Lady Selina. He knew what he might suggest, knew what he could put in place, but the risk to her was great. She met his gaze, looking back at him steadily and, within a few moments, her eyes had widened and her color faded entirely as she somehow realized what he was thinking.

"You would use me," she said, breathlessly. "Is that not so?"

Profound silence filled the room as everyone first turned to Lady Selina and then, with wide eyes and shocked expressions, looked back towards Charles.

"It would be a bet which they would both wish to achieve, and would believe they *could* achieve," he said, reluctantly. "We would have to be on our guard, of course, and make certain that, when they step forward to achieve their goal, they are discovered and shamed for their actions."

"Which would, in turn, leave them to your mercy," Lady Amelia said, as Charles nodded, barely lifting his eyes from Lady Selina. "But why should it be Lady Selina that you use, Barrington? Could I not –"

"Because they have already blackmailed Lord Barrington and have him under their control," Lady Selina interrupted, her voice still quiet, but her eyes no longer holding the shock which he had seen only moments before. "If the bet is placed and it is to do with me, then they will feel as though they are not only able to achieve it, they will be eager to do so, given just how poorly they know I think of them."

"Lord Telford believes that Lady Selina was aware of his involvement with Lord Havers," Charles explained, as the others began to murmur to each other. "He has already attempted to pull her away in order to do the very same with her as he did to Amelia. Of course, he did not succeed, and thus, I believe that he has all the more reason to attempt to take on the bet."

Lady Hayward shook her head.

"I do not like this suggestion," she said, as Lady Selina reached across to put a hand over hers. "It places Lady Selina in great danger."

"But there will be none," Lady Selina replied, before Charles could say anything. "I trust Lord Barrington. I am sure that, if he states that I will be protected and that the sole purpose is to make certain that Lord Havers and Lord Telford are blackmailed in the same way that they also have blackmailed others, then I cannot easily refuse."

Lady Hayward shook her head, but Charles knew that Lady Selina was determined. He himself did not like such an idea and certainly had turned away from it many times in his mind, before realizing, slowly, that there was nothing else for them to do.

"I will make certain that the bet is placed, although under another gentleman's name," he said, slowly, thinking hard. "It will be clear and determined. And I will inform you of it the moment it is done, Lady Selina." She nodded, even though there remained a dark frown on Lady Hayward's face. "I thank you for your trust in me, Lady Selina," Charles finished, gratitude and anxiety twining together within his heart. "Be assured, I will not let you down."

Her smile was warm, her eyes bright.

"I have no doubt of that, Lord Barrington," she said, filling his heart with affection for her all over again. "No doubt at all."

CHAPTER ELEVEN

Selina felt as though every part of her was trembling. Stepping into the ballroom no longer brought her any enjoyment but, instead, only fear.

"I will say it again," Lady Hayward said firmly, as they walked in together. "I do not like this situation."

"And yet, you allow it?"

Lady Hayward shook her head and looked at Selina with a steady gaze.

"I believe that a young lady ought to decide her own future, Lady Selina," she said, quietly. "I am sure that you are aware of that, given what you witnessed with both of your older sisters."

"I am," Selina replied, quietly. "I know that you would not put me in danger, Lady Hayward. And I am grateful to you for permitting me my own choice."

"There is a fondness in your heart for Lord Barrington," Lady Hayward stated, unequivocally. "I believe it is returned. I will confess that I believe it a good match, but

I can also see, in addition, that there must be an end to the matter with Lord Telford before such a thing can even be considered." She shook her head. "Believe me, Lady Selina, I very much hope that Lord Telford will face the consequences of his actions, but I also wish very much that you were not involved."

Selina smiled at her chaperone, trying to hide her own anxiety.

"I am aware of that, Lady Hayward and, truth be told, I find myself thinking the very same. But I am willing to do what I must, in order to bring an end to such a dreadful thing – not only for Lady Amelia's sake but for the other young ladies who might then be set in Lord Telford's path."

Lady Hayward smiled grimly.

"I must hope that all that Lord Barrington and Lord Banfield have planned will work without difficulty," she said, as Selina nodded fervently in agreement. "But as you have said, you must be on your guard against him, Lady Selina. We cannot permit Lord Telford to strike out against you until the situation is set."

"I am aware of that," Selina replied, softly, looking around her. "Have no doubt, Lady Hayward, I will remain close to you and to Lord Barrington, should it be required of me."

"I am glad to hear it." She turned, having started slightly at the sound of Lord Barrington's voice. "But recall, if you will," he continued, "that you must make certain to dance with Lord Telford, should he ask you to do so. I have little doubt that he will seek to build up even a modicum of trust within you. He will return you to Lady Hayward without delay and will not seek to do as he has done in the past."

"You mean to say that you do not think it will be Lord Telford who will attempt to take Selina?" Lady Hayward asked, as Lord Barrington nodded. "But she is not yet introduced to Lord Havers!"

"A matter I expect to be rectified within a few short days," came the reply. "Lord Havers will find a way to make your acquaintance, Lady Selina. I expect that it will be he who attempts to steal you away, when the time comes."

She nodded and hid her shudder.

"Then the bet is placed?" Lady Hayward asked, as Lord Barrington nodded. "Might I ask who wrote it?"

At this, Lord Barrington's face broke into a wide smile. "I have an acquaintance named Lord Donaldson, who hails from Scotland. He is always eager to be involved in any such scheme and, I confess, is inclined to indulge in too much liquor. I spoke to him yesterday afternoon and explained the situation and his part within it. He was very frustrated to hear Lord Telford's scheme and I had to convince him not go towards him at once!" A small chuckle escaped him. "But he was more than willing to do as I asked. The bet has been placed and Lord Telford was present to see it." His smile faded. "I, of course, was not."

"Might I ask the specifics of this bet?" Lady Hayward asked, as Selina laced her fingers in front of her tightly. "What has been said?"

Lord Barrington cleared his throat, perhaps feeling a

trifle awkward. "Lord Donaldson has declared himself to have been rejected by you, Lady Selina," he said, with a small, apologetic smile. "He states he is distraught but also filled with irritation that such a chit of a girl should treat him such a way. The cries he made in Whites, I believe, were heard by almost everyone present!" His smile grew just a little. "He talked of how he expected to be considered by you, how, as an Earl, he did not think himself too lowly, but how you were less than eager to dance with him and converse with him. Given that he was pretending to be in his cups, the fact that he placed a most ridiculous bet was accepted by all."

Selina swallowed hard.

"The bet," she asked, quietly. "What did it say?"

Lord Barrington took a small step closer to her, his voice dropping low.

"Lord Donaldson stated that he was so greatly injured by your rejection that he wants very much to see you similarly injured, rejected by those around you," he said, quietly. "Therefore, to any gentleman who can pull you from your chaperone, who can encourage you into a less than proper situation where Lord Donaldson himself might then happen to see such a thing occur, will be given a great deal of coin from Lord Donaldson."

Lady Hayward shook her head urgently.

"But that might mean, Lord Barrington, that a great *many* gentlemen will be seeking to do such a thing!" she exclaimed, as Selina sucked in a breath into her tight lungs, realizing what her chaperone meant. "Lady Selina is in very great danger!"

"Indeed, it may well appear so, but most gentlemen

of the *ton* will find such a bet most improper and down-right disgraceful," Lord Barrington assured her. "In addition, Lord Donaldson has stated that any gentleman who wishes to take on such a task must inform him of it at once, and of their movements, so that he can make sure that he will be present to see Lady Selina being so compromised. Those who do not will not receive a single penny from him. It has all been written out in great detail and the specifics are quite clear."

A measure of tension left Selina's frame, but the nervousness and anxiety still remained.

"Lord Donaldson will inform either myself or Lady Hayward of the gentlemen who have sought to do as he has asked," Lord Barrington continued, gently. "I do not expect there will be many."

"And, in doing so, he will be able to inform us of Lord Telford's plans," Selina finished, as Lord Barrington nodded. "I quite understand, Lord Barrington."

He inclined his head towards her.

"I will have Lord Donaldson introduce himself to you this evening, albeit in as quiet a manner as possible, given the animosity that is meant to be between you." Reaching out, he touched Selina's hand and she gave it to him at once, feeling the gentle press of his fingers and finding herself a little more encouraged. "You are doing a great deal for Lady Amelia and myself, Lady Selina. I do hope that you know just how grateful I am to you."

"I do it not only for both of you, but also for those who might otherwise have been ruined by Lord Telford's cruelty," Selina replied, squeezing his fingers in return before reluctantly letting them go. "But I should very much like to see you freed from this burden, Lord Barrington."

Grimacing, he shook his head.

"I would pay as much as was asked of me, if it kept my sister – and you also, Lady Selina - safe from harm," he said, fervently, "but it is their cruelty, selfishness and arrogance that I must battle against."

"And it seems we shall do so," Lady Hayward stated, as Lord Barrington allowed himself a small smile. "Let us pray that we are successful."

THERE IS a fondness in your heart for Lord Barrington.

Lady Hayward's words spun around Selina's mind as she waltzed with the very gentlemen in question. She could not deny that there was such a thing, and certainly, it seemed, could not hide it either. The fact that Lady Hayward believed that it was returned to her, that Lord Barrington also had an affection for *her,* was something too wonderful to believe.

And yet, Selina knew that there could be no discussion on such a matter until the situation with Lord Telford could be brought to a close. However, for the moment, she could steal little moments of joy for herself – such as this very moment here.

"You dance very well, Lady Selina."

"I thank you, Lord Barrington," she murmured, all too aware of his nearness as he held her gently. "I do very much enjoy dancing with you."

Shock and embarrassment filled her as she realized

precisely what she had said. There was no escaping from it now. She had *meant* to state that there was nothing she enjoyed more than dancing but had managed to tell him just how much she appreciated *his* company specifically!

"I am honored, Lady Selina," came the reply, as he glanced down at her, probably aware of the flush of mortification which now washed right through her. "And for what it is worth, I would say the very same to you."

Swallowing hard, Selina nodded, smiled briefly and then focused solely on the dance itself. She did not need to say anything more, did not need to embarrass herself further. Evidently, her heart had spoken without her realizing it – but Lord Barrington, it seemed, had not taken either offence or appeared embarrassed. Rather, he was dancing with a small smile on his face and a brightness in his eyes that was unmistakable.

"Thank you, Lady Selina."

Much to her relief, the dance came to a close and she was able to step back from him into a curtsey.

"I am now filled with regret," he continued, offering his arm as they turned to make their way back to Lady Hayward.

"Oh?"

She dared not look at him, wondering now if he had something to say about what she had accidentally said.

"I regret that our dance is at an end, Lady Selina," he said, speaking with such tenderness in his voice that Selina caught her breath, her heart beginning to hammer furiously in her chest. "For I was eagerly anticipating it and now that it is over, I must wait until the next ball before I can dance with you again." He stopped for a moment and looked down at her. Selina swallowed hard as she glanced up into his face, blushing furiously at the look in his eyes. "Say that you will save the waltz for me, Lady Selina," he murmured, so that only she could hear, "at the next ball we attend - you will not allow another gentleman to put his name there?"

Selina did not know what to say, feeling so over-whelmed by his request that she wanted to both laugh aloud with joy and clasp her hands together with delight.

"But of course," she managed to answer, after a few moments, her composure still entirely intact. "I should be glad to do so, Lord Barrington."

The smile on his face spread all the more as he looked back down at her.

"Wonderful," he said, softly. "And now, allow me to return you to Lady Hayward."

Lady Hayward was not alone by the time they reached her. By her side there stood a tall, broad shoul-dered gentleman, with a strong jaw and firm grey eyes. Selina did not know him and wondered who this gentleman might be, only for Lady Hayward to smile at her and gesture towards him.

"Lord Donaldson," she said quietly, as Selina approached. "You are meant to be introduced already, if you recall."

Lord Barrington let go of Selina's hand as she quickly bobbed a curtsey.

"Yes, of course," she replied, wondering if this intimi-dating gentleman was as kind-hearted as Lord Barrington had made out. "We are already meant to be introduced."

"And I am meant to be greatly angered with you,"

Lord Donaldson replied, no smile upon his face. "I thought it best to be seen talking with you briefly, Lady Selina, although in a few moments, I shall storm away and speak with another," he said, as Selina nodded. "I am very sorry to hear that you have not been treated well by Lord Telford, although I understand it is Barrington's sister who has been in the greatest difficulty?"

"That is so, Lord Donaldson," Selina replied, nodding. "I know that Lord Barrington is greatly appreciative of your willingness to assist us."

Lord Donaldson lowered his head for a moment.

"But of course," he said, grimly. "I am glad to have been asked, for such a thing deserves great punishment."

"Have any gentlemen approached you about your bet?" Lord Barrington asked, with Lord Donaldson nodding. "They have? Already?"

"Only one," Lord Donaldson replied, his expression returning to the rather dark look that had been there only moments before. "A Lord Smithfield. I do not know him."

Lord Barrington chuckled, although Selina did not know why, given just how much anxiety was beginning to pile upon her heart.

"I am acquainted with Lord Smithfield," Lord Barrington told them both, a twinkle in his eye. "I can assure you, Lady Selina, that you have nothing to fear from him. He is an older gentleman who has more eagerness than ability, no matter what he sets his mind to."

Selina let out a long breath of relief.

"I see," she said, as Lord Barrington chuckled again. "Then I have nothing to concern myself with at present."

"No, you do not," Lord Donaldson replied, although he still did not smile. "And now, I shall take my leave of you. I must make it quite clear, of course, that you have once more slighted me, Lady Selina."

"I quite understand," Selina replied.

She turned her face sharply away from Lord Donaldson and looked directly across the ballroom so that it appeared that she had no further interest in the man. She heard Lord Barrington laugh under his breath, as Lord Donaldson muttered something about speaking to Lord Barrington again when he had a little more news. And then, he was gone.

"I do not think anyone could mistake your acquaintance with Lord Donaldson as being a positive one," Lady Hayward considered, as Selina smiled at her. "That was very well done."

"I thank you," Selina replied, softly. "Lord Donaldson seems to be an excellent gentleman."

Lord Barrington shook his head, slicing the air between them with his hand.

"Do not allow anyone to hear you say so," he told her, as a flush of embarrassment crashed down upon Selina, making her realize she had been somewhat ill considered in her remark. "And should any young lady seek to ask you questions about Lord Donaldson, then you must make certain to lie."

Selina nodded, dropping her head just a little so that she would not have to look into Lord Barrington's face.

"I understand."

"This requires a great deal of you, I know," Lord

Barrington continued, a good deal more gently. "I am sorry for it, Lady Selina. Would that I could take your place myself!"

"I *must* beg an introduction!" Before Selina could answer, a gentleman came directly to stand by Lord Barrington, whose face immediately went rather pale, followed by a deep, red flush which crept up his neck. "Come now, Barrington!" the gentleman continued, grinning broadly. "I have long been seeking an introduction to the lady and you cannot allow her to escape me now."

Selina frowned, but then quickly wiped the expression from her face. She was meant to be amiable, happy and contented, just as any young lady of the *ton* might be. That meant being eager to know any new acquaintances who sought her out.

"I am not certain that the lady wishes to be introduced to *you*, Lord Havers," Lord Barrington said, and instantly, Selina was on her guard.

She allowed her smile to fall away, permitted her brows to lower and saw how Lord Havers watched her closely, seeing her change of expression.

"It seems as though Lord Telford was correct in his assumption," Lord Havers said, bowing low towards Selina. "You *are* aware of our involvement with Lady Amelia then, Lady Selina."

"I am certainly aware enough to know that I have no wish to be introduced to you, Lord Havers," Selina replied, steeling herself inwardly. "What you did to Lady Amelia is beyond the pale."

The gentleman grinned suddenly, as though he found what Selina said to be most amusing indeed.

"But you are unable to speak of it to anyone," he said, as Selina felt a faint stirring of anger deep within her heart. "Is that not so?"

Selina looked away from Lord Havers, knowing it was best that she ignore him at present. The urge to retort was strong indeed, but she remained silent, having nothing to say to the gentleman.

"I believe this conversation is at an end, Lord Havers," she heard Lord Barrington say, firmly. "Good evening to you."

Lord Havers laughed again and Selina forced herself to look back at him, seeing the dark smile on his face and finding herself caught between anger and deep displeasure.

"I will consider myself now acquainted with you, Lady Selina," he said, bowing low again. "I do hope that you will step out onto the floor with me at the next ball. I would very much like to dance with you."

"I think not," Selina replied, knowing full well that she would have no other choice but to do so, albeit with an apparent and obvious reluctance. "Good evening, Lord Havers."

She waited with her face turned away from his until, after a few moments longer, he finally took his leave. Her shoulders slumped with relief and she let out a long breath, looking up at Lord Barrington and seeing the very same anger in his eyes that she felt within her heart.

"You did very well, Lady Selina," he said, reaching for her hand and pressing it lightly. "I thank you for your willingness in all of this."

"He is the most odious of gentlemen!" Selina

exclaimed, as Lady Hayward nodded fervently, choosing, it seemed, not to notice Lord Barrington's hand upon Selina's. "And so arrogant!"

"Indeed," Lady Hayward agreed, speaking for the first time in some minutes. "And no doubt, he will come to ask you to dance at the next ball, Lady Selina, and you will have to do your utmost to refuse."

Selina smiled ruefully.

"But you, being my eager and most supportive chaperone will encourage me not to display any rudeness of manner nor ill will. Is that not so?"

Lady Hayward laughed and nodded.

"It will be my part to play – albeit reluctantly!" she exclaimed, as Selina smiled back at her. "But it appears as though, thus far, everything is going just as we have anticipated."

She looked towards Lord Barrington, who was beginning to nod slowly.

"Now all we need do is wait," he said, letting go of Selina's hand, who immediately felt a sharp sting of loss. "Lord Donaldson will inform us the moment Lord Havers or Lord Telford speak to him to accept the bet. Thereafter..." He looked at Selina and smiled and she felt her heart calm once more. "Thereafter, it will be all on your shoulders, Lady Selina. Would that I could take it from you but–"

"I am not afraid," Selina replied, a little surprised to note that she spoke the truth, for the anxiety that she had felt, the fear that had burned within her soul, had now left her entirely. When she looked up into Lord Barrington's face, it all seemed to melt away, leaving her to draw in nothing but new-found courage and strength. "I will do what must be done. And Lady Amelia will be free from them for good."

CHAPTER TWELVE

"You *are* going to marry the lady?" Charles looked up, astonished, as Banfield's brow lifted slightly. His heart thumped wildly in his chest as his friend remained silent, clearly waiting for a response to his question and yet it was an answer that Charles found himself almost reluctant to give. "Come now!" Banfield exclaimed, as Charles cleared his throat, feeling a little awkward. "You must know that there is a clear and sincere affection for the lady which is seen in practically everything you do!"

"I do not know...." Charles broke off, closed his eyes and shrugged. "Yes, very well. Lady Selina, for that is whom you are speaking of, has become of significant importance to me of late."

Banfield chuckled and lifted his glass of whisky to take a small sip.

"Great importance?" he repeated, sardonically. "That does not speak of affection, Barrington! Only of practicality."

"Then what do you wish me to say?" Charles asked, finding it rather difficult to begin to express what he truly felt for the lady. "There is – that is to say, I have an awareness that there is something new within my heart, and as yet, I have not fully determined what such a feeling is."

"It is either affection or it is love," Banfield replied, practically. "It can only be one of those two things, I am sure, for there is such an obvious awareness of her presence whenever she is nearby that even I have noted it!"

Charles frowned and ran one hand over his eyes, relieved that they were speaking quietly together within his own townhouse rather than out at White's or in some other public place.

"I can do nothing as yet," he said, slowly. "I must deal with this situation first."

"But of course," Banfield said, waving a hand. "But thereafter, what will you do? Even assuming that we manage this, the fact of the bet will have cast some doubt on her reputation amongst some of the ton – you cannot mean to allow her to suffer for it? Neither do I presume that you will simply let Lady Selina return to that quiet acquaintance which she was at first? What if some other gentleman wishes to court her? Then what would you do?"

"I would not allow that!"

The words shot from Charles' mouth with such force that Banfield's eyes flared with astonishment for a moment before he began to laugh, wiggling one finger in Charles' direction.

"If that is not evidence of your feelings towards the

lady, then I do not know what is," he said, as a flush of embarrassment crept into Charles' face. "You cannot abide the idea of another gentleman courting her. Not when you hope to do so yourself."

Charles considered this carefully, examining his heart and discovering that everything Banfield said was quite correct. He *did* want to court Lady Selina. In fact, he wished for more than that, were he being entirely honest. Even the suggestion that she might be courted by another gentleman sent a bitter taste into his mouth, a hard anger beginning to form within him as he considered it. That was not something he could permit. He would speak to Lady Selina and beg for her consideration before he would allow such a thing to occur!

"She needs to know how you feel and what your intentions are," Banfield said, quietly. "Even if you do not wish to do any more at present – which is quite understandable given what is at hand – she will be glad to know the thoughts and considerations within your heart and mind, Barrington. It will give her hope."

A frown flickered across Charles' brow.

"Hope?"

Again, Banfield grinned, although he shook his head in evident frustration that Charles was seemingly unaware of what he was about to say.

"The lady cares for you also, I am quite sure of it," he said, firmly. "But she does not know the truth of how you feel! Therefore, she considers you and wonders about you and silently prays that something will be said, something will be *done* which will prove to her that her affections and loyalty are not misplaced."

The way Lady Selina had looked into his eyes some two nights ago, when he had taken her hand, the sparkle in her eyes and the joy in her expression, slammed back hard into Charles' mind. He had found himself reaching to take her fingers in his on more than one occasion, his eagerness to protect the lady growing steadily as he did so. Was Banfield correct? Did he need to say something to her, so that she understood what he felt and what he yearned for?

"Consider it, at least," Banfield replied, only to be interrupted by a tap at the door.

"Enter."

Charles waited as the butler stepped in, holding out a silver tray towards him.

"This has only just arrived, my Lord," the butler said, as Charles picked up the sealed note. "There was no expectation of a reply, however."

"I see," Charles murmured, turning the letter over and seeing the seal which he knew to be that of Lord Donaldson. His heart turned over in his chest. "Thank you."

"Might I fetch you anything else, Lord Barrington?"

"No, nothing more at this point."

Charles waited until the door was closed tightly, then gestured to the letter.

"It is from Lord Donaldson."

Banfield was out of his chair in an instant as Charles broke open the seal, his heart hammering at a furious pace as he did so.

"'Lord Telford has informed me that he intends to take on my bet'," Charles read aloud, as Banfield nodded, his expression a little grim. "'At Lord Copeland's ball in two days' time. I am to meet him – or his accomplice – in the green room, where I will be shown proof of their achievement.'"

Charles blew out his breath between flattened lips, feeling both relief and burning anger growing within him.

"Then Lord Telford *does* intend to take on the bet, as we had expected," Banfield murmured, not returning to his chair, but instead beginning to walk up and down the length of Charles' study. "Lady Selina must be informed."

"I will write to her at once," Charles began, only to see his friend frown at him. "That is to say, I shall *call* upon her at once."

"An excellent suggestion," Banfield replied, with a chuckle, lightening the tense atmosphere almost at once. "And who knows? There may be opportunity for you to speak of something other than Lord Telford's plan!"

Charles tried to scowl, but found himself smiling despite himself. Picking up his glass of whisky, he finished the rest and then, folding the letter and placing it inside his pocket, he rose from his chair.

"I think I shall go at once, Banfield. Do excuse me, will you?"

Banfield chuckled.

"But of course," he said, making his way to the door. "I myself have another pressing visit that I must undertake just as soon as I can."

"Oh?"

Charles looked at his friend, who was now standing by the open door, waiting for him.

"With Lady Amelia," Banfield replied, with a broad smile. "She is waiting for me in the drawing room. I did say that I would not be long with you."

With happiness in his heart that his sister had not only found such an excellent gentleman in Banfield but that, in addition, Banfield himself appeared to be so very contented, Charles let a broad smile curve his lips.

"Then I suggest that you hurry," he replied, walking smartly towards the door. "And Banfield, if you have not done so already, then might I suggest that you tell her the truth of what is in your heart?" He shrugged and gestured with his hands, spreading them wide. "The true depth of feeling that is held there, you understand. I know for certain that she will appreciate hearing such a thing from you – or, at least, I have been told that she will do so!"

Grinning at Banfield, he could not help but laugh at his friend's wry expression and, stepping out of his study, made his way quickly towards the front door.

"You are quite certain?"

Charles nodded, taking the letter out of his pocket, unfolding it and handing it to Lady Selina, who took it at once. She read it quickly, then handed it to Lady Hayward who also read it without hesitation. When she looked up, her expression was grim and Charles felt a small stab of guilt within his heart. He was asking a great deal of Lady Selina, he knew, but she was, it seemed, more than willing to help him. She had always been so, right from the very beginning of her acquaintance with Lady Amelia, when she had gone to her aid without Lady Amelia ever truly realizing that she required it.

"You will be able to speak to your father, I hope?" Charles asked, as Lady Selina nodded fervently. "And he will do as we ask?"

"I am sure of it," Lady Selina replied, with such firmness in her voice that Charles could not help but smile. "He may very well wish to know all that I intend to do, and might very well demand that I tell him all, but should he do so, then I have no qualms about speaking the truth to him. And I have little doubt that he will be most displeased and upset, but that he will, in the end, understand that I am in no particular danger."

"No, you will not be," Charles promised, as Lady Hayward sighed and rose from her chair, her fingers twining together as she held them in front of her, making her way across the room to ring the bell. "You will be watched closely, Lady Selina, and every moment you spend with Lord Havers or Lord Telford, depending on who seeks you out, will be observed. You will never be without help, should they change their intentions."

She nodded slowly and Lady Hayward turned to look back at Charles directly, although she did not sit down.

"Do you believe that they trust Lord Donaldson's bet?" she asked, as Charles spread his hands. "Might Lady Selina be in even more danger than we thought?"

Charles wanted to lie, to state that he was quite certain that Lord Telford believed every word of Lord Donaldson's bet, but to do so would be entirely disingenuous, and he did not want to express any such thing to the lady.

"I cannot say for certain, Lady Hayward, for I do not know the thoughts and considerations agreed between the two gentlemen. However, what I will state is that it is now well known that Lady Selina has rejected Lord Donaldson entirely and, given the outward appearance of both Lord Donaldson and Lady Selina when they first talked at the ball some two days ago, I think that belief has become all the more acknowledged. That is, perhaps, why Lord Telford has now decided to take on Lord Donaldson's bet."

"Because he believes that all Lord Donaldson has said is true," Lady Selina murmured, as Charles nodded. "That does make a good deal of sense, Lady Hayward."

Lady Hayward nodded, her eyes searching Charles' face for a moment or two before she sighed.

"Very well," she said, softly. "Let us pray that the Duke himself will be just as considerate and understanding, should he have to be informed of it all."

"Indeed," Charles agreed, smiling just a little.

He looked back at Lady Selina and saw her watching him, her eyes bright despite the nervousness he knew she must be feeling. The urge to say just how much he had come to admire her grew within his heart but, with Lady Hayward present, Charles found himself reticent.

"I must go and chase up that maid!" Lady Hayward said suddenly, as though she somehow knew that Charles had more that he wished to say, but that he did not want to do so when she was present. "I will be but a few moments."

Lady Selina's eyes widened in surprise.

"The maid will be coming very soon, Lady Hayward," she said, as her companion made her way to the door. "I am sure that–"

"A few moments!" Lady Hayward replied, waving a hand before stepping out of the door, leaving it wide open.

Charles smiled a little self-consciously before looking back at Lady Selina, who had only just realized, it seemed, why Lady Hayward had left the room. Her cheeks began to infuse with color and she dropped her gaze to her hands as they rested gently in her lap.

"You must know just how greatly I admire you, Lady Selina." Charles had thought it would be very difficult indeed to speak the truth to Lady Selina but, as he began, he found his words coming with ease and purpose, as though he was eager to speak them to her. "I want to assure you that I will not allow any harm to come to you."

"I trust you entirely, Lord Barrington," she replied, as he smiled at her, seeing the way her eyes darted to his and then jumped away again. "There is nothing that I fear which, I might add, is rather remarkable."

He tilted his head just a little.

"Oh?"

Her blush deepened.

"I have always been rather quiet," she told him, speaking slowly as if she needed to choose her words with great care. "My twin sister, Anna, has always been the one to speak first, to allow the *ton* to become aware of her presence. She has a confidence that I myself have lacked, and that I have, in addition, sought desperately for myself."

A small frown caught Charles' brow.

"You do not lack confidence, Lady Selina."

"It may not appear so, Lord Barrington, but I have felt it slowly increasing within me as our acquaintance has gone on," she told him, surprising him. "When I first came to London, I felt nothing but anxiety and tension when it came to any social occasion. I was, in fact, even considering returning to my father's estate, given just how poorly I knew I fared. However, Lady Hayward has been the most stalwart of companions and made certain that I came to understand that my desire to be as my sister is was not an ideal which I needed to reach."

"What do you mean?" Charles asked, finding himself all the more intrigued with the lady. "You felt the urge to replicate your sister's behavior?"

She nodded.

"That is it precisely, Lord Barrington. But Lady Hayward has encouraged me to be as I truly am, without any requirement to hide my character away. She was correct." Her smile lit up her eyes. "I have found a confidence within myself that has been brought about solely by my acquaintance with both you and Lady Amelia, Lord Barrington. I have found myself struggling with fear and tension but have stepped out of their grasp and faced things that I dread with a confidence which I have never experienced before. And now that I am to face Lord Telford, being fully aware of his plans, I find that I do not have that same fear any longer." She smiled at him, her eyes dazzling him with their beauty. "I am certain that much of my assurance comes from the knowledge that you will be watching me, Lord Barrington. That you will step in when it is required, that you will not allow me to come to harm."

"And that I will beg of you to remain by my side when the time comes." The words hung in the air between them for a moment and, as Charles watched the lady, he saw how her brows flickered, how a line formed gently between them. Did she realize what he meant? Emboldened, he continued quickly, wanting to speak honestly before Lady Hayward returned. "Lady Selina, it is true that I will do all I can to protect you," he said, urgently, "but it is more than that. There is a great affection for you within my heart, Lady Selina. Once this matter is brought to a close, once Lord Telford and Lord Havers are brought low, I will have a matter of urgency still heavy upon my shoulders."

He was surprised to hear just how swiftly she caught her breath but, studying her face, he was sure that it came from a place of hope and of expectation, rather than anxiety or worry.

"A matter of...?"

"I should not like to speak out of turn," he continued quickly, aware that Lady Hayward could return at any moment. "But I must be frank, Lady Selina. I – I do care for you - deeply."

Those last few words had been a little stuttered and Charles found himself now struggling for breath, as though it had taken all of his energy to speak of such a thing to her. As he looked directly into Lady Selina's eyes, Charles felt his heart lift with joy as a beautiful smile began to spread across her face. It lifted her expression entirely, her eyes sparkling with evident happiness, her cheeks still gently flushed with color. She had never looked more beautiful.

"You speak the truth?"

He nodded fervently.

"I do," he said, his voice a little softer than before. "I speak it with great eagerness also, Lady Selina, for I wish you to know of my intentions."

"And they are?"

Her smile was a little teasing now, her head tilting to the left just a little. Charles laughed and she laughed along with him, both sharing in the happiness which seemed to wrap itself around them.

"I should like to court you, Lady Selina," he said, after a moment. "Of course, I am aware that I will need to speak to the Duke himself, and I will be glad to do so, but only if you would be happy for me to do so."

She let out a long sigh, although her smile did not diminish.

"I should be very happy indeed, Lord Barrington," she answered, as Charles closed his eyes for a moment and took a deep breath, feeling the last strands of tension leave his frame. "For what you have spoken of is within my heart also."

It was at that very moment that Lady Hayward decided to make a reappearance, her footsteps breaking any further conversation between Charles and Lady

Selina. But the smiles that they shared spoke of the joy that now settled in each of their hearts, and despite all that faced them both, Charles truly believed that he had never felt such a happiness as this before.

CHAPTER THIRTEEN

S peaking to her father about the matter at hand had
not been an easy task.

Selina had deliberately kept many things from him,
knowing in her heart that he would refuse to permit her
to attend the ball that evening should she tell him everything. Lady Hayward had been present with her at the
time of the discussion and Selina had not missed the
frown which had crossed her chaperone's brow upon
occasion. She herself was greatly appreciative of Lady
Hayward's willingness to allow her to continue as she
had planned, although she was also fully aware that the
lady would have stepped forward and refused outright
had she any great concerns over Selina's safety. As things
stood, there was a clear plan ahead of them, one which
made certain that Selina herself would not be left alone
at any time, even if Lord Telford or Lord Havers believed
her to be so.

"And so, if I recall correctly, I am to go with Lord
Banfield at a time of his choosing?" the Duke said, as the

carriage rumbled on its way towards the ball. "To a particular room?" He frowned. "I do not fully understand."

"I know you do not, Father," Selina replied, gently. "All will become clear, but I assure you it is for a worthy cause."

The Duke harrumphed, but said very little in response.

Selina had told him of the difficulty with Lady Amelia, whom she now considered a particular friend and had, in addition, spoken at length of Lord Barrington. Her father had shown a little interest in that, which, Selina knew, was entirely to her advantage. When she had told him of the blackmail and all that Lord Havers and Lord Telford were attempting to do, she had seen the dark anger flash in his eyes and had felt her heart swell with both relief and admiration for her father.

The fact that he was not a particularly effusive father did not mean that he lacked compassion for anyone in trouble. His expectations for the behavior of gentlemen were fixed, and his outrage at hearing that Lady Amelia had been treated so poorly was entirely genuine. Selina had not told him the details of what would occur this evening, but had stated that his presence as a Duke was required at a certain time, and that Lord Banfield – whom her father had been introduced to on a previous occasion – would be the one to fetch him. Her father was, of course, intending to make his way to the card room almost at once, having no interest in dancing or the like, but he had promised to go with Lord Banfield the moment it was required.

"And this Lord Barrington of yours, Selina," her father said abruptly, as the carriage began to slow. "Once this matter with his sister is at an end, I believe that he and I are to converse on a particular subject!" Selina caught her breath, staring across the carriage at her father and barely able to make out his features in the dim light. "He wrote to me," her father explained, speaking a little more gently but with a smile in his voice. "He has requested to call at my earliest convenience. I am sure that you must know what it is he wishes to speak to me about?"

"I – I do, Father," Selina replied, her voice a little thin, such was her surprise at hearing that Lord Barrington had been so eager. "You do not think to refuse him, I hope?"

The Duke laughed loudly and slapped his knee, making Selina smile with relief.

"Refuse an Earl?" he asked, as chuckles still escaped from him. "A gentleman who is more than suitable for my daughter and who, according to Lady Hayward, has been *most* attentive to you?" He shook his head as the carriage door was opened. "No, my dear Selina. I shall not refuse him. I only hope that he will continue to prove himself worthy."

"I have no doubt that he will, Father," Selina replied, her whole being flooded once more with happiness and relief. "Thank you."

"LADY SELINA."

Selina felt herself stiffen at once as she heard the voice of Lord Havers near her. She did not turn around but rather remained precisely where she was, waiting for the moment to pass. Would Lord Havers insist on coming to speak to her? Would he insist on dancing with her, as he had already said he would do? Part of her struggled with the idea of being in his company for so long but, of course, she knew that she had no other choice. If the plan was to go ahead, then she had to make a show of being unwilling to dance with him whilst evidently being aware that she had no other choice.

"Lady Hayward."

The tightness in her frame did not leave her as Selina turned her head to see Lord Havers bowing towards Lady Hayward. He had chosen his moment well, for she stood in a small group of gentlemen and ladies, who were all conversing with each other. To refuse him a dance now would mean making her dislike of the gentleman obvious and to do such a thing would, she was sure, only bring trouble and difficulty for Lady Amelia.

"You do recall our introduction, I hope?" Lord Havers continued, as Selina narrowed her eyes just a fraction. "I had hoped to peruse your dance card, Lady Selina."

Hearing the small murmur of conversation from the others within the group, Selina let out a slow breath and lifted her chin.

"I do believe you will already be aware of my answer, Lord Havers," she said, speaking so quietly that she was sure he would have to strain to hear her. "Why you should ask me such a thing again, I cannot imagine."

"Because I simply *must* be permitted to dance with you, Lady Selina," he replied, with another sharp inclination of his head. "Pray do not make me beg, Lady Selina, although I shall do such a thing if it is required. You will find me quite determined."

"Lord Havers, good evening!"" came the voice of one of the young ladies in the group, who had clearly been listening to what was said, given the sharp look in her eye. "Are you seeking a dance partner for this evening?" She gestured to the others who stood nearby. "I am sure that you will find many a willing young lady here."

Lord Havers chuckled and bowed again.

"Miss Lindale, you are very kind," he said, with a smile that did not reach his eyes. "I shall be certain to ask as many as wish it from me, once I have chosen a dance from Lady Selina's card."

Selina closed her eyes for a moment, her lips pulling flat as Lord Havers grinned back at her, very aware of the situation he had put her in. With great reluctance, she handed him her dance card and he practically snatched it from her fingers, before hurriedly writing his name in not one but two spaces. With a triumphant look, he handed it back to her and Selina took it from him, hiding her satisfaction. Thankfully, Lord Barrington had written his name down for the waltz, which meant that Lord Havers had been required to choose from some of the others – although Selina was certain that he would have taken the waltz, had he been able to.

"And the first of our dances is to be in only a moment!" Lord Havers exclaimed, looking delightedly at her. "The cotillion. Now, if you will excuse me for a

moment, Lady Selina, I must go and ask Miss Lindale for
her dance card, which I am sure she will give me without
any sort of reluctance."

Selina remained silent until he had made his way
past her, before turning to glance at Lady Hayward.

"The cotillion and then the country dance," she said,
slowly. "I cannot tell which one he means to –"

"We did not expect him to pick two dances," Lady
Hayward murmured, as Selina shook her head. "The
cotillion is a very busy dance indeed. I am sure that Lord
Barrington will be stepping out to dance it also."

Selina swallowed hard and nodded, feeling a small
swirl of fear begin to wrap itself around her heart. They
had not expected Lord Havers to write his name down
for two of her dances and, thus, she was now uncertain as
to which one he intended to bear her away from once it
had come to an end.

"There is no time for me to speak to Lord Barrington," she said, realizing that the cotillion was only
minutes away. "What shall we do, Lady Hayward?"

Lady Hayward smiled gently.

"Lord Barrington has been near to you this entire
evening," she said, quietly. "Can you not see him?"

Startled, Selina looked all about her but saw nothing
but strangers and acquaintances, only to suddenly catch
sight of his familiar face looking directly back at her. He
was standing with Lady Amelia and their mother, with
Lord Banfield just to Lady Amelia's left. With a ques-
tioning look on his face, his brow began to lower and
Selina gave him a sharp nod, praying that he understood.

"I think it will be this dance," she said hurriedly, as

the dancers from the previous dance began to make their way back from the floor. "At present, there is nowhere for me to go to escape him. I have no other choice *but* to dance with him. However, for the second dance which is some time away, I might choose to avoid him – and therefore, the dance – entirely."

Lady Hayward's eyes lit.

"Indeed, that is true," she said, reaching out to press Selina's hand. "It would be easy enough to slip away for the country dance. Lord Havers cannot risk you doing so."

"Therefore, it will be this one," Selina replied, just as Lord Havers turned back towards her. "It is, as you have said, a very busy dance indeed."

Lady Hayward squeezed her fingers again and then let Selina's hand go.

"Be careful," she said, urgently. "Be on your guard."

Nodding, Selina looked up to see Lord Havers grinning broadly at her, although the darkness in his eyes frightened her somewhat.

"The dance is about to begin, Lady Selina," he said, as Selina steeled herself inwardly. "Shall we step out onto the floor?"

"If I must," Selina replied, not wanting to pretend that she was quite content with the situation at present but making her dislike quite clear.

She ignored the offer of his arm and walked out onto the dance floor, with Lord Havers quickly falling into step with her. Rather than allowing her to remain near to Lady Hayward, however, he led the way across the room to the opposite side of the dance floor, where they joined other couples ready to form a set. The dance was, as Selina had expected, very busy indeed and, after only a few moments, she could not see Lady Hayward at all, such were the number of couples lining up to dance.

"I do hope that you enjoy this dance, Lady Selina," Lord Havers said, as the music began and he bowed towards her. "I am certain that I shall."

She did not reply but instead kept her face turned just a little away from him, although she did drop into a very quick curtsey, as was expected. The ladies stepped forward and Selina calmly began to dance the required steps, but inwardly, her heart was beating at a furious pace as she felt her anticipation and nervousness begin to rise steadily within her. Lord Havers watched her with a sharp eye, a small smile on his lips throughout the entirety of the dance, and Selina felt her stomach twist. She could give him no awareness that she knew of what he planned. She had to act accordingly, when he made his move, had to make every appearance of fright and dismay. Only then would he believe himself to be fully in control.

The music finally, blessedly, came to an end and Selina curtsied towards Lord Havers again, knowing that she would have to take his arm this time. He, in due course, offered it to her and, after a momentary hesitation, she took it.

"Now, Lady Selina," he said, as they began to meander slowly back through the crowd. "I have an acquaintance whom I am sure you are aware of." Selina kept her mouth firmly closed, although she noted that he was beginning to veer to the right, away from where Lady

Hayward was waiting. "Lord Telford?" Lord Havers continued, quickly. "He was greatly displeased to learn that you were the one who spoke to Lord Barrington about his involvement in a particular situation with Barrington's sister." Her stomach still twisting in a tight knot, Selina kept her gaze straight ahead and still chose to say nothing. "Lord Telford and I have gained a good deal of coin from Lord Barrington and, given his interest in you, I believe that he might be willing to give us a little more, should something similar happen to you." Selina's skin crawled and she attempted to remove her hand from his arm, only for Lord Havers to reach across and grasp it with his own. "Now, if you struggle and attempt to go anywhere other than remaining by my side, Lady Selina," Lord Havers continued, his voice now low and grating hard across her skin, "I shall bend my head and kiss you in the most improper manner. And then what will become of your reputation?"

"I..."

She hoped that her hesitant word sounded convincing. Her breathing was coming quick and fast as Selina forced herself to remain precisely where she was, even though everything within her was crying out to step away from him, to run away from this situation. Praying silently that she would have enough strength to continue and fixing her mind solely upon Lord Barrington, Selina walked alongside Lord Havers and allowed him to lead her forward.

"Now, we are to walk together to another small room and there, Lady Selina, you will wait until Lord Barrington is brought to you," Lord Havers continued.

"Your reputation will be sullied enough in the *ton*'s eyes to find you in a room alone with a gentleman – and Lord Barrington will know that also. He will pay whatever is demanded. I have no doubt about that."

"You are despicable."

Selina's whispered words only caused Lord Havers to laugh cruelly, as though he found her quite ridiculous. Biting her lip, Selina steadied her breathing as best she could and reminded herself that, as she had been dancing, all manner of things had been occurring. Lord Banfield would have fetched her father. Lady Hayward, Lady Amelia and Lady Barrington would have waited together to watch her dance, to make certain of where she was, and Lord Barrington himself would now be following her, albeit at a distance. She had no need to worry. Everything would be just as they had planned.

"Through here, if you please." Selina caught her breath as he gestured to a door which led them away from the ballroom. Looking all about her, she let out a quiet yelp of pain as Lord Havers pushed her bodily through the door, before grasping her arm in a tight grip. "And then through here," he said, pushing open a door and thrusting her inside.

Selina stumbled in, with Lord Havers letting out a cry of laughter, which faded away in an instant as the door behind him was shut tight, closing them into the room, and none other than Selina's father rose from his chair, his eyes wide with horror.

"Father!" Selina went to him at once, wanting to reassure him that she was not injured. "You were summoned, then?"

"I was," the Duke replied, although his eyes remained fixed on Lord Havers who was now beginning to back away towards the door. He turned, only for Lady Hayward and Lady Barrington to move to stand in front of it, barring his way. He could not leave now, other than by physically moving both ladies aside, which Selina knew he would not do.

"Explain to me what has just occurred, Selina!" the Duke exclaimed, putting one hand out to her. "Why did this gentleman thrust you into this room in such a fashion? I thought that—"

"Lord Havers and Lord Telford have been determined to do to me what they did to Lady Amelia, Father," Selina explained, as the Duke's face slowly infused with color. "Lord Havers told me so explicitly."

The Duke drew in a long breath, his shoulders lifting.

"Is that so, Lord Havers?" he bellowed, as the gentleman shrank back, no trace of his arrogant nature present any longer. "You thought to *shame* my daughter in order to force money from me?"

Selina turned to face Lord Havers, her confidence beginning to overflow now that she was quite safe with her father, Lady Hayward, and Lady Barrington.

"I believe, Lord Havers, that you are the one who now finds himself trapped," she said, lifting her chin. "Now be seated. Lord Telford is due to arrive at any moment and I am sure that both you and he will be required to give a long and detailed explanation to my father, the Duke of Landon."

She glanced up at her father and saw the glimmer of anger in his eye, wondering if he knew that she had arranged this precisely so that he would be able to bring his judgement down upon these two gentlemen.

Lord Havers said nothing, but sat down heavily, before putting his head in his hands and his elbows on his knees, as though he wanted to hide himself away before them all. Selina let out her breath slowly, feeling a great sense of relief rush through her. All they required now was Lord Telford's presence and, thereafter, this matter would come to a swift and decisive end.

CHAPTER FOURTEEN

"Lord Barrington."

Charles, who had, before returning to the ball-room himself, made certain that Lady Selina had been brought to the green room by Lord Havers, turned his head to look directly into the eyes of Lord Telford.

"I have nothing to say to you, Telford," he stated, before making to leave. "Good evening."

The gentleman reached to grasp Charles' arm, and it was all Charles could do not to physically push him away.

"I would not walk away from me, Lord Barrington, if I were you" Lord Telford said, with a grim smile. "Not when Lady Selina is, at present, in much the same situation as your sister recently was."

Charles felt his stomach twist, a sense of victory already rising up within him as he forced a dark frown to furrow his forehead.

"What do you mean, Telford?"

Lord Telford chuckled.

"You have not heard of the bet, then?" he said, airily. "Lord Donaldson, it seems, has been slighted by Lady Selina and, as such, has begged for someone to slight *her* in much the same way – a way guaranteed to see her rejected by much of society." He shrugged one shoulder. "It seemed the perfect opportunity to not only win the bet, but also to make certain that *you* increased your payment to us significantly."

Setting his jaw, Charles glared at the man.

"And why should I do such a thing?"

"Come now!" Lord Telford laughed, folding his arms across his chest. "You are not going to deny that you care for Lady Selina, I hope?" His laugh came again and Charles' gritted his teeth, truly irritated by the man's demeanor. "I know that you will do whatever you can to save her reputation. And, in which case, I must ask you to join me at this very moment in order to *rescue* her from Lord Havers."

"I swear, Telford, if you have placed one finger upon her, then –"

"I have no time for your threats," Lord Telford replied, with a weary look. "Do hurry up, Barrington. I am sure that she is eagerly waiting for you."

Charles glanced all around him and then followed the gentleman. Lord Donaldson, he hoped, had already been informed by Lord Telford that he had managed to succeed and that, therefore, Lord Donaldson himself would be present in the room. Recalling just in time that he was not meant to know where Lord Telford was leading him, Charles hung back rather than striding forward, glaring at the gentleman as he held back a door for him.

"Just to your left, Lord Barrington," Lord Telford said, with a half bow as though he were a servant. "There you will find –"

"Lead on, Lord Telford," Charles interrupted, darkly. "If you believe that I am about to step inside whilst you remain out here, you are sorely mistaken. There are things I wish to say to both yourself and to Lord Havers, for I can assure you that I have no intention of paying anything more."

This seemed to shock Lord Telford somewhat, for the smile slipped from his face and he hesitated where he stood. And then, after a moment, he shrugged and stepped forward.

"Very well," he said, airily. "If you believe that Lady Selina is not present, then you are quite wrong, Lord Barrington."

He pushed the door open and stepped inside, with Charles following quickly so that the gentleman could not escape.

One step into the room, Lord Telford came to a dead stop, his hand still on the door handle. Charles, unwilling to wait for fear that Lord Telford would turn and attempt to flee, pushed the gentleman bodily into the room, before pushing the door shut and standing against it so that no-one could escape. With great satisfaction, he looked about the room and took in the scene before him. Lord Havers, hunched on a chair, his head in his hands, Lord Donaldson was standing by Lord Banfield, with both Lady Hayward and his mother sitting quietly together just behind him. The Duke of Landon was on his feet, his face red with anger and his hands clenched into fists. Lady Selina was standing by the Duke's side, with a small smile on her face as she met Charles' eyes. And Amelia, who was a little pale, sat close to where Lady Selina stood, her hands in her lap but with a look of great relief etched across her face.

"It seems that we have managed to achieve our aim," Charles said, his voice filling the room. "You see, Lord Telford, Lord Donaldson has not been slighted by Lady Selina, as you might have believed. In fact, he is very eager to make certain that both you and Lord Havers are no longer permitted to do anything such as this again!"

Lord Telford half turned, only for a quiet groan to come from Lord Havers. He, at least, appeared to realize that there was nothing more they could do.

"You mean to say, Lord Barrington, that both Lord Telford and Lord Havers, having already done such a cruel thing to Lady Amelia, now turned their attention to *my daughter?*"

These last words were practically shouted, filling the room with the Duke's vehemence.

"I knew that they were attempting this, father," Lady Selina said, her voice a gentle wind to the Duke's furious outburst. "But I could not tell you, for it had to be proven. You had to see it with your own eyes, for then consequences could be brought to these gentlemen for what they had tried to do."

"It would have been no good with merely hearsay," Lady Hayward added, looking steadily back at the Duke who had slowly begun to loosen his tight fists, clearly becoming a little calmer. "You had to know the truth of what these gentlemen were doing. You had to see it for yourself."

"And so I have done," the Duke grated, his voice low and his expression one of utter rage. "You attempted to force my daughter into a situation where her reputation would have been at stake, solely for your own gain." He held up one hand as Lord Telford began to stammer. "You need not attempt to find any excuses, Lord Telford. I am fully aware of what you have done to Lady Amelia and what you have demanded of her brother. For you to think that you could demand the same from me is even further beyond the pale!"

Lord Havers lifted his head and looked at Lord Telford, and Charles found himself very satisfied indeed with the look of sheer despair on the gentleman's face. They had been outwitted and Charles was very glad of it, for now not only was his sister safe from any further demands, the two gentlemen would not be able to carry out their scheme against any other young ladies of the *ton* either.

"There will be consequences for this," the Duke continued, as Charles nodded fervently. "Have no doubt, gentlemen. I will make quite certain of it!"

"As will I," Charles added, as both Lord Banfield and Lord Donaldson said the same. "You will find yourselves removed from society entirely, gentlemen."

Lord Telford lifted his chin, although there was a paleness about his lips that betrayed his ongoing dismay.

"What will you do?" he asked, as though this was nothing more than foolishness. "If you tell any others about what has occurred, then you risk your sister's reputation, Lord Barrington!"

Charles' mouth lifted in a half smile and he took a small step towards Lord Telford.

"Lady Amelia is to be wed very soon," he said, calmly. "She has found the most excellent of gentlemen and will not be injured in the slightest by what I might have to say to the *beau monde* of your cruel attempts to manipulate her." He gestured towards the Duke. "And do you truly believe that His Grace would do anything to jeopardize the reputation of his daughter?"

The Duke's jaw tightened.

"I should think not," he grated, as Lord Telford's shoulders dropped and his head lowered. "But surely you must realize that, as a Duke of the realm, there are a great many things which I am able to influence. Many things that I am able to say. And certainly, a great deal that I can do to make sure that you will *never* be able to lift your heads in society again!"

This seemed to finally defeat Lord Telford, for a groan escaped his lips as he ran one hand over his eyes. Lord Havers remained where he was, his head in his hands again and a great heaviness about his frame.

"Might I suggest that the rest of us depart and leave Lord Telford and Lord Havers to consider their actions?" Charles remarked, as a bright, contented smile spread across Lady Selina's face. "Our task has come to an end. The ball is still in full swing and I, for one, feel cause to celebrate."

"As do I," Lady Hayward replied, taking Charles' mother's arm. Lady Barrington drew close to Charles and reached up to kiss his cheek, her eyes damp but a watery smile on her lips. Reassuring her quietly that all was well and that there was nothing further to fear, he thanked Lady Hayward for her part and watched them exit the room.

"I think," the Duke said, as the others came close to him, "that I might remain for a time, Lord Barrington."

Charles nodded, seeing how both Lord Telford and Lord Havers stiffened.

"But of course, Your Grace."

"There are a few things I wish to say specifically to these gentlemen," the Duke continued, gesturing for his daughter to go with Charles. "Thank you, Barrington."

"Of course." Charles offered Lady Selina his arm, as Banfield offered Lady Amelia his, and together, they left the room. The door closed tightly behind them and Charles let out a long breath, smiling first at his sister and then at Lady Selina. "It is done," he said, as they both smiled back at him. "It is over. And now there is nothing left to block our way."

THE FOLLOWING AFTERNOON, Charles found himself sitting in the drawing room with both Lady Selina and Lady Hayward, looking at them both and finding his heart so filled with relief that it was difficult to find the words to express it.

"How does the Duke fare?" he asked, as Lady Selina exchanged a quick glance with her chaperone.

"His Grace and I had a long discussion," Lady

Hayward said, a slight strain about her eyes. "Lady Selina was present also, of course, and I believe that he understands why things were done in such a specific way."

Charles frowned, wondering if the Duke had questioned Lady Hayward's actions.

"I hope it was not a difficult conversation," he said slowly, as Lady Hayward again looked to her charge. "I am sorry if it was troubling."

"It was difficult," Lady Selina replied, with a small shrug. "My father did not want me to be at risk in any way, and yet that was the very reason I did not explain everything to him at the first." She rose and made her way to ring the bell for tea. "He was very angry, of course, but it was not directed towards myself or Lady Hayward. Rather, it was entirely towards Lord Havers and Lord Telford. Once he realized just how safe I had been throughout the entirety of last evening, he became a little more calm, and expressed his gratitude about how well it had all been managed." Her expression softened. "I know he is eager to speak to you also, Lord Barrington."

"As I am with him, I assure you!" Charles replied, speaking honestly and feeling his heart swell with love as he looked into Lady Selina's eyes. "You did very well last evening, Lady Selina. I am all the more in awe of your courage and fortitude."

"That courage and fortitude only existed within me due to your presence nearby," she replied, swiftly. "To know that you were there, that you were watching me, and making certain that I would not come to harm, brought me all the strength which I required."

Charles smiled at her and, with a quick glance

towards Lady Hayward, felt himself grow hot with the words that he wished to say to Lady Selina, but which he could not, given Lady Hayward's presence.

"I must beg you to excuse me for a moment!" Lady Hayward rose suddenly. "I have left my needlework in the library and must have it at once!"

Lady Selina frowned.

"Surely a maid can...."

She trailed off, glancing towards Charles before color began to rise in her cheeks. Lady Hayward chuckled and then made her way to the door.

"I will be but a few minutes, Lord Barrington," she said, in a warning tone. "Do be wise."

Charles nodded and immediately turned again to Lady Selina, whose pink cheeks only brought him a swell of gladness in his heart. She knew what he wanted to say, surely?

"Lady Selina, the matter with my sister and Lord Telford is now at an end," he said, pushing himself from his chair and coming to stand before her. Holding out one hand to her, he waited until she had taken it before he gently pulled her to her feet, aware that she was closer to him than ever before. Her golden hair curled gently around her temples like a crown, her eyes were bright with hope and happiness.

"I will speak to your father very soon," he continued, softly, "but before I do so, I want you to know the truth of my heart."

"Speak it, Lord Barrington," came the gentle reply. "I would know of it."

He took in a deep breath, a little surprised at how much nervousness climbed through his veins.

"It is to tell you, Lady Selina, that my heart no longer holds an affection for you." Seeing the smile fade from her face, the startled look that came into her eyes, he spoke more quickly. "That is to say that mere affection has been replaced by a deep and ever-growing love for you. A love which, I am quite certain, will not be removed from my heart, but will linger there for the rest of my days. I cannot be without you, Lady Selina. I cannot even *consider* my life without your presence. I seek to court you, yes, but if I can, I will make it of such a short duration that we shall find ourselves betrothed within the week!"

For a moment, Lady Selina appeared so startled that words were stolen from her lips. Her eyes were wide, her color heightened still and then, after a few moments longer, she began to laugh.

"A week?" she asked, as he smiled down at her, his hand still in hers. "A week is much too long, Lord Barrington." Boldly, she moved a little closer to him, her eyes still fixed to his. "When there are two hearts so similar to each other, when there is a bond already being forged which cannot be broken, it is a great burden to have to endure a week of courtship when we both long for something more."

His heart swelled and he caught her about the waist, her hands quickly going around his neck.

"You are the most wonderful of ladies," he told her, softly. "The most courageous, caring, kind-hearted and generous creature I have ever had the opportunity to know. How could I not be drawn to your beauty?" Bending his head, he caught her lips for the briefest of moments, not daring to do more, but yet unable to stop himself. "I love you, Selina."

"As I love you," came her sweet reply as Charles held her close and clasped her to his heart.

Aw, I love to see a happy ever after! I hope you enjoyed their story! The next book in the series is on preorder, A Christmas Match.

Want something more to read right now? Please check out one of my favorite series, The Spinsters Guild, and start with A New Beginning

A SNEAK PEAK OF A NEW
BEGINNING

CHAPTER ONE

"Good evening, Miss Taylor."

Miss Emily Taylor, daughter to the Viscount Chesterton, kept her gaze low to the ground, her stomach knotting. The gentleman who had greeted her was, at this present moment, looking at her with something akin to a leer, his balding head already gleaming in the candlelight.

"Good evening, Lord Smithton," she murmured, hearing the grunt from her father than indicated she should be doing more than simply acknowledging the gentleman's presence. The last thing Emily wished to do, however, was to encourage the man any further. He was, to her eyes, grotesque, and certainly not a suitable match for someone who had only recently made her debut, even *if* he was a Marquess.

"Emily is delighted to see you this evening," her father said, giving Emily a small push forward. "I am certain she will be glad to dance with you whenever you wish!"

Emily closed her eyes, resisting the urge to step back

from the fellow, in the knowledge that should she do so, her father would make certain that consequences would follow. She could not bring herself to speak, almost feeling Lord Smithton's eyes roving over her form as she opened her eyes and kept her gaze low.

"You know very well that I would be more than pleased to accompany you to the floor," Lord Smithton said, his voice low and filled with apparent longing. Emily suppressed a shudder, forcing herself to put her hand out and let her dance card drop from her wrist. Lord Smithton, however, did not grasp her dance card but took her hand in his, making a gasp escape from her mouth. The swift intake of breath from behind her informed Emily that she was not alone in her surprise and shock, for her mother also was clearly very upset that Lord Smithton had behaved in such an improper fashion. Her father, however, said nothing and, in the silence that followed, allowed himself a small chuckle.

Emily wanted to weep. It was obvious that her father was not about to say a single word about Lord Smithton's improper behavior. Instead, it seemed he was encouraging it. Her heart ached with the sorrow that came from having a father who cared so little for her that he would allow impropriety in front of so many of the *beau monde.* Her reputation could be stained from such a thing, whispers spread about her, and yet her father would stand by and allow them to go about her without even a twinge of concern.

Most likely, this was because his intention was for Emily to wed Lord Smithton. It had been something Emily had begun to suspect during these last two weeks, for Lord Smithton had been present at the same social gatherings as she had attended with her parents, and her father had always insisted that she greet him. Nothing had been said as yet, however, which came as something of a relief, but deep down, Emily feared that her father would simply announce one day that she was engaged to the old, leering Lord Smithton.

"Wonderful," Lord Smithton murmured, finally letting go of Emily's hand and grasping her dance card. "I see that you have no others as yet, Miss Taylor."

"We have only just arrived," said Emily's mother, from just behind Emily. "That is why –"

"I am certain that Lord Smithton does not need to know such things," Lord Chesterton interrupted, silencing Emily's mother immediately. "He is clearly grateful that Emily has not yet had her head turned by any other gentleman as yet."

Closing her eyes tightly, Emily forced herself to breathe normally, aware of how Lord Smithton chuckled at this. She did not have any feelings of attraction or even fondness for Lord Smithton but yet her father was stating outright that she was interested in Lord Smithton's attentions!

"I have chosen the quadrille, the waltz and the supper dance, Miss Taylor."

Emily's eyes shot open, and she practically jerked back the dance card from Lord Smithton's hands, preventing him from finishing writing his name in the final space. Her father stiffened beside her, her mother gasping in shock, but Emily did not allow either reaction to prevent her from keeping her dance card away from Lord Smithton.

"I am afraid I cannot permit such a thing, Lord Smithton," she told him plainly, her voice shaking as she struggled to find the confidence to speak with the strength she needed. "Three dances would, as you know, send many a tongue wagging and I cannot allow such a thing to happen. I am quite certain you will understand." She lifted her chin, her stomach twisting this way and that in fright as Lord Smithton narrowed his eyes and glared at her.

"My daughter is quite correct, Lord Smithton," Lady Chesterton added, settling a cold hand on Emily's shoulder. "Three dances are, as you know, something that the *ton* will notice and discuss without dissention."

Emily held her breath, seeing how her father and Lord Smithton exchanged a glance. Her eyes began to burn with unshed tears but she did not allow a single one to fall. She was trying to be strong, was she not? Therefore, she could not allow herself to show Lord Smithton even a single sign of weakness.

"I suppose that is to be understood," Lord Smithton said, eventually, forcing a breath of relief to escape from Emily's chest, weakening her. "Given that I have not made my intentions towards you clear, Miss Taylor."

The weakness within her grew all the more. "Intentions?" she repeated, seeing the slow smile spreading across Lord Smithton's face and feeling almost sick with the horror of what was to come.

Lord Smithton took a step closer to her and reached for her hand, which Emily was powerless to refuse. His eyes were fixed on hers, his tongue running across his lower lip for a moment before he spoke.

"Your father and I have been in discussions as regards your dowry and the like, Miss Taylor," he explained, his hand tightening on hers. "We should come to an agreement very soon, I am certain of it."

Emily closed her eyes tightly, feeling her mother's hand still resting on her shoulder and forcing herself to focus on it, to feel the support that she needed to manage this moment and all the emotions that came with it.

"We shall be wed before Season's end," Lord Smithton finished, grandly, as though Emily would be delighted with such news. "We shall be happy and content, shall we not, Miss Taylor?"

The lump in Emily's throat prevented her from saying anything. She wanted to tell Lord Smithton that he had not even asked her to wed him, had not considered her answer, but the words would not come to her lips. Of course, she would have no choice in the matter. Her father would make certain of that.

"You are speechless, of course," Lord Smithton chuckled, as her father grunted his approval. "I know that this will come as something of a surprise that I have denied myself towards marrying someone such as you, but I have no doubt that we shall get along rather famously." His chuckle became dark, his hand tightening on hers until it became almost painful. "You are an obedient sort, are you not?"

"She is," Emily heard her father say, as she opened her eyes to see Lord Smithton's gaze running over her form. She had little doubt as to what he was referring to, for her mother had already spoken to her about what a husband would require from his wife, and the very thought terrified her.

"Take her, now."

Lord Smithton let go of Emily's hand and gestured towards Lady Chesterton, as though she were his to order about.

"Take her to seek some refreshment. She looks somewhat pale." He laughed and then turned away to speak to Emily's father again, leaving Emily and her mother standing together.

Emily's breathing was becoming ragged, her heart trembling within her as she struggled to fight against the dark clouds that were filling her heart and mind. To be married to such an odious gentleman as Lord Smithton was utterly terrifying. She would have no joy in her life any longer, not even an ounce of happiness in her daily living. Was this her doing? Was it because she had not been strong enough to stand up to her own father and refuse to do as he asked? Her hands clenched hard, her eyes closing tightly as she fought to contain the sheer agony that was deep within her heart.

"My dear girl, I am so dreadfully sorry."

Lady Chesterton touched her arm but Emily jerked away, her eyes opening. "I cannot marry Lord Smithton, Mama."

"You have no choice," Lady Chesterton replied, sadly, her own eyes glistening. "I have tried to speak to your father but you know the sort of gentleman he is."

"Then I shall run away," Emily stated, fighting against the desperation that filled her. "I cannot remain."

Lady Chesterton said nothing for a moment or two, allowing Emily to realize the stupidity of what she had said. There was no-one else to whom she could turn to, no-one else to whom she might escape. The only choices that were open to her were either to do as her father asked or to find another who might marry her instead – and the latter gave her very little hope.

Unless Lord Havisham....

The thought was pushed out of her mind before she could begin to consider it. She had become acquainted with Lord Havisham over the few weeks she had been in London and he had appeared very attentive. He always sought her out to seek a dance or two, found her conversation engaging and had even called upon her on more than one occasion. But to ask him to consider marrying her was something that Emily simply could not contemplate. He would think her rude, foolish and entirely improper, particularly when she could not be certain that he had any true affection for her.

But if you do nothing, then Lord Smithton will have his way.

"Emily."

Her mother's voice pulled her back to where she stood, seeing the pity and the helplessness in her mother's eyes and finding herself filling with despair as she considered her future.

"I do not want to marry Lord Smithton," Emily said again, tremulously. "He is improper, rude and I find myself afraid of him." She saw her mother drop her head, clearly struggling to find any words to encourage Emily. "What am I to do, mama?"

"I – I do not know." Lady Chesterton looked up slowly, a single tear running down her cheek. "I would save you from this if I could, Emily but there is nothing I can do or say that will prevent your father from forcing this upon you."

Emily felt as though a vast, dark chasm had opened up underneath her feet, pulling her down into it until she could barely breathe. The shadows seemed to fill her lungs, reaching in to tug at her heart until it beat so quickly that she felt as though she might faint.

"I must go," Emily whispered, reaching out to grasp her mother's hand for a moment. "I need a few minutes alone." She did not wait for her mother to say anything, to give her consent or refusal, but hurried away without so much as a backward look. She walked blindly through the crowd of guests, not looking to the left or to the right but rather straight ahead, fixing her gaze on her goal. The open doors that led to the dark gardens.

The cool night air brushed at her hot cheeks but Emily barely noticed. Wrapping her arms about her waist, she hurried down the steps and then sped across the grass, not staying on the paths that wound through the gardens themselves. She did not know where she was going, only that she needed to find a small, dark, quiet space where she might allow herself to think and to cry without being seen.

She soon found it. A small arbor kept her enclosed as she sank down onto the small wooden bench. No sound other than that of strains of music and laughter from the ballroom reached her ears. Leaning forward, Emily felt herself begin to crumble from within, her heart aching and her mind filled with despair. There was no way out. There was nothing she could do. She would have to marry Lord Smithton and, in doing so, would bring herself more sadness and pain than she had ever felt before.

There was no-one to rescue her. There was no-one to save her. She was completely and utterly alone.

CHAPTER TWO

Three days later and Emily had stopped her weeping and was now staring at herself in the mirror, taking in the paleness of her cheeks and the dullness of her eyes.

Her father had only just now informed her that she was to be wed by the Season's end and was now to consider herself engaged. There had been no discussion. There had been not even a thought as to what she herself might feel as regarded Lord Smithton. It had simply been a matter of course. She was to do as her father had directed, as she had been taught to do.

Emily swallowed hard, closing her eyes tightly as another wave of tears crashed against her closed lids. Was this to be her end? Married to Lord Smithton, a gentleman whom she despised, and allowing herself to be treated in any way he chose? It would be a continuation of her life as it was now. No consideration, no thought was given to her. Expected to do as she was instructed without question – and no doubt the consequences would be severe for her if she did not do as Lord Smithton expected.

A shudder ran through her and Emily opened her eyes. For the first time, a small flickering flame of anger ignited and began to burn within her. Was she simply going to allow this to be her life? Was she merely going to step aside and allow Lord Smithton and her father to come to this arrangement without her acceptance? Was she truly as weak as all that?

Heat climbed up her spine and into her face. Weak was a word to describe her, yes. She *was* weak. She had tried, upon occasion, to do as she pleased instead of what her father had demanded of her and the punishment each time had broken her spirit all the more until she had not even a single thought about disobeying him. It had been what had led to this circumstance. If she had been stronger, if she had been more willing to accept the consequences of refusing to obey her father without question without allowing such a thing to break her spirit, then would she be as she was now?

"Then mayhap there is a time yet to change my circumstances."

The voice that came from her was weak and tremulous but with a lift of her chin, Emily told herself that she needed to try and find some courage if she was to find any hope of escaping Lord Smithton. And the only thought she had was that of Lord Havisham.

Viscount Havisham was, of course, lower in title and wealth than the Marquess of Smithton, but that did not matter to Emily. They had discovered a growing acquaintance between them, even though it was not often that

her father had let her alone to dance and converse with
another gentleman. It had been a blessing that the
requests to call upon her had come at a time when her
father had been resting from the events of the previous
evening, for her and her mother had been able to arrange
for him to call when Lord Chesterton had been gone
from the house. However, nothing of consequence had
ever been shared between them and he certainly had not,
as yet, made his request to court her but mayhap it had
simply been too soon for such a decision. Regardless,
Emily could not pretend that they did not enjoy a
comfortable acquaintance, with easy conversation and
many warm glances shared between them. In truth, her
heart fluttered whenever she laid eyes upon him, for his
handsome features and his broad smile had a profound
effect upon her.

It was her only chance to escape from Lord Smithton.
She had to speak to Lord Havisham and lay her heart
bare. She had to trust that he too had a fondness for her,
in the same way that she had found her affections
touched by him. Else what else was she to do?

Lifting her chin, Emily closed her eyes and took in a
long breath to steady herself. After a moment of quiet
reflection, she rose and made her way to the writing table
in the corner of the bedchamber, sitting down carefully
and picking up her quill.

～

"Miss Taylor."

Emily's breath caught as she looked up into Lord

Havisham's face. His dark blue eyes held a hint of concern, his smile somewhat tensed as he bowed in greeting.

"Lord Havisham," she breathed, finding even his very presence to be overwhelming. "You received my note, then."

"I did," he replied, with a quick smile, although a frown began to furrow his brow. "You said that it was of the utmost importance that we spoke this evening."

Emily nodded, looking about her and seeing that her father was making his way up the small staircase towards the card room, walking alongside Lord Smithton. Their engagement was to be announced later this evening and Emily knew she had to speak to Lord Havisham before that occurred.

"I know this is most untoward, but might we speak in private?" she asked, reaching out and surreptitiously putting her hand on his arm, battling against the fear of impropriety. She had done this much, she told herself. Therefore, all she had to do was continue on as she had begun and her courage might be rewarded.

Lord Havisham hesitated. "That may be a little...."

Emily blushed furiously, knowing that to speak alone with a gentleman was not at all correct, for it could bring damaging consequences to them both – but for her, at this moment, she did not find it to be a particularly concerning issue, given that she was to be married to Lord Smithton if he did not do anything.

"It is of the greatest importance, as I have said," she replied, quickly, praying that he would consent. "Please, Lord Havisham, it will not take up more than a few minutes of your time." Seeing him hesitate even more, she bit her lip. "Surely you must know me well enough to know that I would not force you into anything, Lord Havisham," she pleaded, noting how his eyes darted away from hers, a slight flush now in his cheeks. "There is enough of a friendship between us, is there not?"

Lord Havisham nodded and then sighed "I am sorry, Miss Taylor," he replied, quietly, looking at her. "You are quite right. Come. The gardens will be quiet."

Walking away from her mother – who did not do anything to hinder Emily's departure, Emily felt such an overwhelming sense of relief that it was all she could do to keep her composure. Surely Lord Havisham, with his goodness and kind nature, would see the struggle that faced her and seek to do what he could to bring her aid? Surely he had something of an affection in his heart for her? But would it be enough?

"Now," Lord Havisham began, as they stepped outside. "What is it that troubles you so, Miss Taylor?"

Now that it came to it, Emily found her mouth going dry and her heart pounding so furiously that she could barely speak. She looked up at Lord Havisham, seeing his features only slightly in the darkness of the evening and found herself desperately trying to say even a single word.

"It is....." Closing her eyes, she halted and dragged in air, knowing that she was making a complete cake of herself.

"I am to be wed to Lord Smithton," she managed to say, her words tumbling over each other in an attempt to be spoken. "I have no wish to marry him but my father insists upon it." Opening her eyes, she glanced warily up at Lord Havisham and saw his expression freeze.

FIND out what happens next between Emily and Lord Havisham in the book available in the Kindle Store A New Beginning

MY DEAR READER

Thank you for reading and supporting my books! I hope this story brought you some escape from the real world into the always captivating Regency world. A good story, especially one with a happy ending, just brightens your day and makes you feel good! If you enjoyed the book, would you leave a review on Amazon? Reviews are always appreciated.

Below is a complete list of all my books! Why not click and see if one of them can keep you entertained for a few hours?

The Duke's Daughters Series
The Duke's Daughters: A Sweet Regency Romance
Boxset
A Rogue for a Lady
My Restless Earl
Rescued by an Earl
In the Arms of an Earl
The Reluctant Marquess (Prequel)

A Smithfield Market Regency Romance
The Smithfield Market Romances: A Sweet Regency
Romance Boxset
The Rogue's Flower

Saved by the Scoundrel
Mending the Duke
The Baron's Malady

The Returned Lords of Grosvenor Square
The Returned Lords of Grosvenor Square: A Regency
Romance Boxset
The Waiting Bride
The Long Return
The Duke's Saving Grace
A New Home for the Duke

The Spinsters Guild
A New Beginning
The Disgraced Bride
A Gentleman's Revenge
A Foolish Wager
A Lord Undone

Convenient Arrangements
A Broken Betrothal
In Search of Love
Wed in Disgrace
Betrayal and Lies
A Past to Forget
Engaged to a Friend

Landon House
Mistaken for a Rake
A Selfish Heart
A Love Unbroken

Christmas Stories
Love and Christmas Wishes: Three Regency Romance
Novellas
A Family for Christmas
Mistletoe Magic: A Regency Romance
Home for Christmas Series Page

Happy Reading!
All my love,
Rose

Made in the USA
Middletown, DE
08 April 2021

37220845R00139